A Slow,
Soft River

7.

A Slow, Soft River

Seven Stories

by

LAWRENCE DORR

edited and introduced by
CORBIN SCOTT CARNELL

WILLIAM B. EERDMANS PUBLISHING COMPANY
Grand Rapids, Michigan

Library of Congress Catalog Card Number 72-94606
ISBN 0-8028-1498-0

Printed in the United States of America

The author wishes to thank the following publications, in whose pages some of these stories first appeared, for permission to include them in this book:

The Virginia Quarterly Review: "Brindley," appearing in the Autumn 1958 issue; "Brandenburg Concerto," appearing in the Autumn 1963 issue; and "Once You Were No People," appearing in the Winter 1967 issue.

The Florida Quarterly: "Curfew," appearing in the Summer 1967 issue; "An Act of Admiration," appearing in the Spring 1967 issue; and "The Binge," appearing in the Winter 1970 issue.

TO
EDWARD FRANCIS WILKINSON
with a grateful heart

Contents

Introduction

Dr. Samuel Johnson once confessed to Boswell that "the biographical part of literature is what I love most." Yet for decades the biographical approach to literary criticism has been considered heresy. Some 19th-century critics did overuse the personalist approach, but the logical end of "objective criticism" is to reduce the artistic creation to an interesting but dead artifact. Many I-Thou possibilities are thwarted if we try to avoid the personality behind the work. In the long run, we seek to glimpse the special consciousness in and behind the work of art, for there is something strangely satisfying in so discovering another human being.

The fiction of Lawrence Dorr is particularly enhanced by knowing something about the author. I discovered this through a class in modern fiction, where after his visit the students were even more interested in reading his work and found new depths of meaning in his stories.

There are artists whose work is so personal and whose inner health is so radiant that meeting them extends the work of art in mysterious ways. The impact of many contemporary artists has been greatly increased through television, recordings, and film. That this should happen suggests two things to me: the electric media are helping to create new potentialities for bringing artist and public together; and knowing about the artist can tap that pool of images and memories sometimes called the collective unconscious in ways which enhance the work of art by facilitating a deeper plunge into the pool. It is impossible to say what is objective and what is subjective in such a process. We look at a person's face when he speaks to us — the work of art is like a face, but we respond to more than the face as our humanity is addressed.

Since Lawrence Dorr prefers to be known by that pen name, I will refer to him only by his real first name, "Janos" (pronounced "YAH-nosh"), and though I omit his last name at his request, I will try to include here the most important biographical data. To begin with, he is one of the most alive people I've ever known. He is an uncommon combination of the active and contemplative, the rash and the prudent, the rational and the strikingly intuitive. His stories well up out of the troubled springs of memory and desire, springs that go deep down into primal sources. And it is significant that he describes fiction writing as a purging of pain. "When something bothers me, haunts or troubles me," he once told a group of writers, "I find I can live with the memory better after I have worked it into a story."

Janos is no stranger to the deeper pains which human beings have known: the violent death of close kin, exile, poverty, war, loss of occupation, and loss of faith. He was born in Budapest, the son of a well-established Hungarian family. He had polio as a child and was educated for a time by governesses and his French mother. His father died when he was seventeen. He entered the

Hungarian equivalent of West Point and on graduation became a first lieutenant in the army. He had expected to live the life of a gentleman with art history as his avocation but instead found himself serving on the Eastern Front during World War II. In 1947, two years after the war was over, he left Hungary as a political exile, and for the next three years worked at odd jobs all over the Continent and England. Some stability and peace came into his life again in 1950 when he married Clare, whom he describes as half-English and half-South Carolinian.

Yet this summary of dark happenings lightened only by marriage could be overlaid with another summary which sounds like the adventures of a fun-loving picaro: frightening off maids and governesses with indoor target practice as a boy, learning the correct way to serenade a girl, writing "trash novels" for spending money (in Hungarian — literally "novels sold under canvas" in curbside shops), tales that were banned by his parents from their household. His adventures as an exile in Europe sound like material for a television rogue-on-the-road series. Who else has worked as a masseur in a Salzburg "entertainment" house, performed with a circus as the front half of a zebra, served briefly in the French Foreign Legion, been a janitor, coal miner, and cotton mill worker, and between jobs been kept alive by feminine kindness?

In all these adventures, however, the artist's mind was collecting impressions and brooding over the glass of memory, composing images to expunge the awful loneliness and sense of loss. By sixteen Janos had written his first novel, the story of a brave soldier named Colonel Lawrence (he liked the name because he liked T. E. Lawrence). As a young man he had written poetry in German

11

and Hungarian and worked briefly for a Hungarian newspaper. He had read Dostoevsky, Tolstoy, and Chekhov in Hungarian, Hemingway in German, and Apollinaire and Cocteau in French.

But it was not until his immigration to the U.S. that he had an opportunity to study American literature. Three months after their marriage, Janos and Clare came from England to Philadelphia, where Janos worked as a copyboy on the *Evening Bulletin* and studied American culture in a special program for internationals at Swarthmore. During this time he discovered an enthusiasm for an author who remains his favorite, William Faulkner. Soon after the birth of their daughter, Janos and Clare responded to an interest which was not new to them, missionary work. Clare was the daughter of Anglican missionaries to Nigeria, and Janos, though unclear in his beliefs, felt eager to do something constructive after a decade of war and wandering. And so they went to the Christian Service Training Center at Frostproof, Florida, which was headed at the time by Dr. Frank Dickinson, an agricultural missionary returned from China.

This religious community was an avant-garde outpost in rural Florida of the early 1950's. To the culture-shock of life in the New World was added exposure to poor-white prejudice, dialect, and suspicion of the foreigner. Yet Janos came to love his "red-neck" (poor white) brethren as well as his black brothers and to make himself understood in broken English. His experiences in Frostproof taught him about growing squash and onions and raising beef cattle and he tried hard in those years to practice Christianity, though Christ at that time seemed far off. When this religious community folded, Janos and his family moved to Sebring, where he worked briefly as a cowboy. Following a back injury (which gets reflected in the story "Brindley"), the family settled in 1955 in the Coconut Grove area of Miami, where Clare worked as an occupational therapist in a local hospital. During the 50's Janos' literary interests were sustained in part through his friendship with British-born Griffin Taylor, who was a published writer.

After what Janos calls his son-of-the-soil years in south-central Florida, he did a variety of jobs in Miami: hospital orderly ("Courage helps."), houseman in a hotel ("Such a job is less awkward in a more traditional country like England."), and as artist's model ("It seems odd but modelling has been the most continuous occupation of my life other than writing."). And while baby-sitting with daughter Sibet and newly arrived John Lawrence, Janos decided to be a free-lance writer. Working on an old typewriter, in a rundown, un-air-conditioned bungalow, he wrote three full novels in less than six years.

The second of these, *The Open Face of Heaven,* was published in 1959 in a German translation (which the publisher called *Wie Diese Schuhe,* or *As Those Shoes*). Partly because the German publisher paid in pounds, Janos and his family decided to visit England, where they spent almost two years with Clare's parents in the fishing village of Beer on the Devon coast. It was during this time that Janos became increasingly close to Clare's father, a retired priest who still served small countryside churches. The warmth and wisdom of his father-in-law, to whom this collection of stories is dedicated, drew Janos steadily toward an orthodox Christianity which he had feared he could no longer accept.

13

The landscape of that part of Devon on the English Channel, the summer-villa country of his youth near Budapest, and the "windy rise" of land on which Janos and Clare have built a house not far from Gainesville, Florida, become a composite Eden in his fiction. Other places in Europe seem forgotten as havens of beauty compared with these spots.

On their return to the United States, Clare took a job as an occupational therapist at the University of Florida Teaching Hospital and in 1962 the family moved to Gainesville, where they have lived since. For several years Janos attended creative-writing seminars with Smith Kirkpatrick of the University's English Department. Through these he met Andrew Lytle and others with whom he had stimulating and helpful exchange. The volume of his writing decreased, but his capacity for careful revision and polishing increased. He also experimented with the ordering of time and point of view, as well as with the challenging task of being affirmative in an un-affirmative age. He worked now primarily on short stories rather than novels.

Janos continued to delight in English as a literary medium, for it seemed to him not to have any ordained literary tone, to have great flexibility, variety, and strength. Having written fiction and poetry in Hungarian, French, and German, he found himself most at home with English. Today he works on the editorial staff of the University's Institute of Food and Agricultural Sciences, "correcting the natives' English," as he is fond of saying.

That he knows six languages (Italian and Russian need to be included also, though he never wrote in these) and remembers his way across cultures is only partial indication of Janos' phenomenal memory — an asset which serves him in everything he writes. He has a memory for small detail: names of obscure places, a scent on the breeze one late afternoon in a village near Budapest, a girl's profile as she carried her baby brother down a Vienna street, the sound of the water below a Devonshire cliff. He is aware of many things simultaneously, and I know of no one so truly oriented in phenomenological reality who also finds in all kinds of phenomena moments of divine transcendence.

His pilgrimage toward God is along a winding river, through flood and nighttime foreboding — a journey in desolate solitude yet with moments of joy and exuberance along the way. Unlike Whitehead's sense of man's progression — from God as Void, to God as Enemy, to God as Companion — Janos begins with God as Companion. He grew up in a home where the father was strong, accomplished, and very loving — where there was the security of many relations and servants. His mother was musical and artistic; his father had a military bearing, a love of fine animals, and the affection of even his subordinates. Not that his home was without tensions. The mother saw herself as a civilizing influence, and the father saw himself as her contact with reality. She was a devout Roman Catholic, he was Reformed. Janos followed his father into the Reformed Church, his sister followed her mother. But despite such differences, it was a happy family. And this strong base of love and respect would help him to keep his sanity under siege in battle, in prison camp, or living the life of a social outcast in cultures that did not know he was a gentleman.

Thus God was never a void. But on the death of his

father, Janos lost God as Companion, knowing the anguish of Peter in "The Binge." God became the Enemy, the implacable Mystery who deals destruction and death as well as love and life. For years, he says, he almost hated God for taking his father, and it seems to me that this quarrel and the closeness to the father forms one of the richest veins in his writing.

If one reads these stories in the order in which they appear here (which is approximately the order of their writing), he will see a pilgrimage unfold. It is a pilgrimage beginning with the discovery of guilt in a barrier erected between father and son ("An Act of Admiration") — a barrier erected by pride, self-will, and misunderstanding; in such a subtle interweaving of motives, who could unravel them? Despite a certain innocence on the part of both father and son, tragedy ensues, as if our inability to comprehend how such brokenness starts epitomizes our living as fallen men. If we could truly understand the origin of fallenness, then perhaps we could correct the situation, but our not comprehending is precisely part of the fall.

In "The Binge" the self becomes fugitive, running from the Almighty Father and trying frantically to hold onto the human father. Then follows the plunge into Woman-Love for solace, release, and the joy of manhood ("Curfew"). In "Brandenburg Concerto" personal sorrow over the loss of the father and separation from family find their parallel in the larger upheavals and injustice of war — and yet at the end there is mercy and reunion. In "Brindley" the mystery of cosmic evil manifests itself in the blind force of a bull and in further senseless loss (another death in the family). The protagonist (here called Andre) questions the inexorability of his situation only to be answered by a greater sense of mystery — yet the reader feels that Andre will be answered.

In "Once You Were No People" the past gets remembered and relived in a way that enables good to work backward into the midst of old pains and ghosts so that new relationships emerge. Memory in the light of newly discovered good extends that good so that mercy, charity, peace — which were there all along — get recognized this time. But as the final story, "A Slow, Soft River," makes clear, this is no mind-over-matter procedure. It is rather a dynamic and untidy process whereby eternity impinges more and more on time until time experiences are remade and go on being remade. This is possible ultimately because it is not human engineering which creates life; real life is being borne along on the River, and once the traveler discovers that he is being borne, the twists and turns, the little cataracts, the snakes in the trees, the "coincidental" offers of acceptance, warmth, even sacrifice are all seen in a different light.

Janos has an amazing sense of all life as Gift. He is one of the few Christians I know whose lifestyle says clearly that he believes in Grace. (I know others, and sometimes find myself among them, who argue against Pelagian works-righteousness and then work themselves to frazzled irritability, all sense of leisure and trustful mirth gone.) Janos knows how to receive gracefully because he finds receiving Grace-ful. Yet there is none of the such-a-worm-as-I kind of humility. He loves himself simply as one of God's creatures — after all, his father and mother loved him too; is their affection to count for nothing? Moreover, if memory keeps finding signs of mercy, how can one

17

doubt God's love? When he gives thanks with fellow Christians in St. Michael's Episcopal Church, whether it be at the Sunday morning Eucharist or at the Wednesday evening healing service, for Janos it is unfeigned thanksgiving.

Stylistically there are many excellent things in these stories. Perhaps most striking is the strong sense of rhythm and sonority. Janos likes, on his own admission, "to sing in prose." Yet he never uses sound for its own sake. He employs it to create dialogue that sounds somehow the way people really speak, to convey central meanings by an aura of what is not said directly but rather overheard in the music of a passage.

In "Brandenburg Concerto" he translates some of the power and rhythm of Bach's music into phrases and clauses.

> He [the soldier] sat on a boxcar's floor with his legs outstretched, leaning against the wall wrapped in one of the Brandenburg concertos, feeling content. The music was alive and intimate and nothing else existed beyond it.

The soldier hears the music in his head, for he is far from any instrument, phonograph, or radio. He lets the music cover him like a canopy, shielding him from the realities of war. Thus he is angry for a moment at the girl who speaks to him, for her voice shuts off the music, causing him to "limp with the rhythm of the boxcar." It is no wonder these stories read well aloud. And in speaking of the role of sound in writing, Janos says, "If I can't hear it in my head, I'm afraid it won't ring true." I can find no false notes in this fiction, so uncanny is his ear for the phoney.

What this storyteller chooses to leave out is another excellence of his style. He knows the good writer doesn't need to set the stage completely, doesn't need to add characters for any purpose but what is organic to his story, doesn't need to turn on the tremolo of emotional generalization which nudges the reader toward one fixed response. There an amazing economy in these stories, for though their author learned English after he was an adult, he never feels the need to parade vocabulary or to overwrite, as Joseph Conrad or Vladimir Nabokov occasionally do. Janos often creates characters by means of vivid metaphors which say what some writers would require sentences to say: the young Jewish girl from Auschwitz who runs "like a stray dog, with her head turned back every third or fourth step"; the old woman who carries her lost son's photograph in her hand "like a sick bird"; the bayoneting soldier who "worked with the not-too-slow, not-too-fast pace of a woodcutter."

There is also a convincing cinematic quality in Dorr's style. It is easy to see that he is a film fan, and college-age readers have responded to his cinematic kind of exposition. I know of one student cinema group making a film based on "Curfew."

But perhaps the strongest thing about these stories is their quality of affirmation. We live in a time when readers have been conditioned to accept bizarre violence, sadistic sex, the most cynical statements about the possibility of meaning and goodness. If a writer creates a genuinely good man, shows self-sacrifice or compassion in action, he is automatically vulnerable to the charge of sentimentality. The irony is that our age is truly sentimental about violence, perverted love, and man's destructive capacities — giving to them a larger place in the arts than any previous age. We seem afraid of goodness, unable to believe anyone has the imagination to really love another. We see ourselves, at least in the arts, as incapable of accepting the initiatives of good.

Lawrence Dorr has seen enough of evil to be a bitter man. He still mourns the loss of loved ones (though I've never heard him mention the loss of property). Loss and pain, however, are only part of the data of experience and he wants to do justice to some of the other data, whether or not it is fashionable right now to do so in fiction. His affirmations are not those of the reformer who creates a world in the abstract and keeps on reforming it in the abstract. His phenomenological sense is too strong for that. He does not affirm cognitive answers so much as images of healing, security, and love (a woman's warm body, a gentle river, bright yellow cookies). The background against which events are realized is not a manipulated one, designed to play down horrors or unfairness. Injustice exists, it even seems to triumph, yet love is operative, with a passion and serenity that is usually not rendered directly but which is overheard, understated, implied in some almost casual line like "Tell me your name."

As the protagonist (usually called Peter or Andre) progresses in his pilgrimage, the stories become more explicit in their Christianity. Janos feels that if Malamud or Roth can be Jewish writers, Sartre existentialist, why can't some be Christian writers? In a world that becomes more secular every day, perhaps Christians will soon be regarded like any other minority. Perhaps we shall one day grant to artists the freedom to speak as believers without automatically accusing them of propaganda.

Introduction

Janos writes increasingly about liberation, about the good news that there is love that is constant, that is not earned, that gives us our freedom. Being a committed Christian makes writing harder, he has found, for in his case it has increased his sense of responsibility. I think he discharges that responsibility well.

> — Corbin Scott Carnell
> *English and Humanities Faculty*
> *University of Florida (Gainesville)*

1

An Act of Admiration

I was fifteen the summer of '36. To me Hitler was no more than the stub of a pencil held to my upper lip to make my sister laugh. This was the summer of the Berlin Olympic Games, of Jesse Owens.

As usual in the summer, we were at our villa fifty kilometres from Budapest. Standing on our front terrace, we could see the Danube, wide and olive green. Four kilometres upriver the far side belonged to the Czechs. I could not see them, but I knew that they were there. I was never allowed to forget, at home or at school, that in 1920 at Trianon a slice of Hungary had been given to the Czechs. That summer the Czechs themselves would not let me forget it. A Czech station was beaming a Hungarian language broadcast telling me that I'd better stop dreaming and wake up to the fact that not one grain of Czech soil would ever be handed back to Hungary. No one else in the house listened to it. I sat alone in the room with its cheerful blue peasant furniture and hand-painted plates and jugs, hating the traitor's sneering voice. On the terrace I could see Mother with a Tyrolean straw hat on her head cutting flowers, and I could hear the guests shouting back and forth to each other as they lay in deck chairs under large striped umbrellas, playing a memory game. They talked endlessly about music and art. They were not interested in Justice and Honor.

Near the staircase leading to the upper rooms, the guns, rifles and carbines, hung against green felt. Solomon, Father's retriever, slept under this staircase. In his sleep he looked as wise as the plaster casts of philosophers at school. We were both waiting for the guests to leave, to have Father back with us: his real self in boots and cord breeches and khaki shirt, following Solomon in the woods, teaching me to walk quietly, to observe and even to smell things. After we had shot and skinned the meat we would sit awhile, he smoking a cigarette and I scratching Solomon's head, and he would tell me about the War.

The sneering voice stopped, and there began a babble in Czech. I turned off the radio and went upstairs and out through the back door across the bridge that led to the back terraces. There was nobody to share my hate. I walked up to the red water tank and climbed on top. I used to play Tarzan here, jumping off the tank to catch the nearest branch of the walnut, but with the sneering voice in my ears I didn't feel like

24

Tarzan. I wondered if I were brave enough to offer my life for my country like Father did, but I wasn't sure. Then I heard Peter whistle our signal, and I jumped off the water tank. Peter was my best friend in the summer. He had accepted me even though I was three years younger and I didn't smoke or earn money. He was the only boy in the village who called me by my Christian name. The others always shut up when I came along.

"I thought you'd gone deaf," he said, standing at the other side of the fence.

"Come over."

He climbed the fence. He was a head shorter than I, and blond, with almost white patches where the sun had bleached his hair.

"I saw you standing on top of the water tank," he said, sitting down on a stump. "Were you playing Tarzan?"

"No. I don't play anymore."

"That's good. Only little boys play. You are as big as a horse." He watched me from the corner of his eyes. I couldn't hit him because he would go off and leave me. Besides, Father told me one didn't hit anyone weaker than one's self. I didn't say anything.

"I've been away." He plucked out a blade of grass and looked at it.

"Where?"

"I don't know if I should tell you."

"You don't have to." I sat down to make myself smaller.

25

"I will if you promise not to tell anybody."

"On my honor." We shook hands.

"I've been away in training with Captain Feher," he said. I burst out laughing.

"Don't laugh. He is a very good captain."

"How can Mr. Feher be a real captain like Father?"

"Not a captain like him," Peter agreed. "Captain Feher is only a Free Corps captain, but he knows how to fight. We are going over tonight."

I stood up. "Across the river?"

"Yes."

"Have you got a uniform and all?"

"Yes. And we are paid much more than the regular soldiers."

"Tonight?"

"Tonight," he said.

"I am going with you. You know I can hit anything with a .22."

"You are too young, Laszlo. We won't be shooting at rabbits; we'll be shooting at Czech soldiers."

"They are much bigger."

"You can't come. You haven't been trained. There isn't any uniform for you." With his arms out he looked like Cicero in our history book.

"Peter, you go and tell Mr. Feher that I am going with him because–"

"You can't just send messages to Captain Feher."

"– because he'll need me. I've been over twice. I wanted to see how they look."

"Did you see them?"

"No, but I saw their pillboxes from a distance. You can't see them from our side. I know where they are. Tell Mr. Feher that I don't want any pay, but I'll need a rifle."

"Can't you bring one with you?"

"No. I'd have to ask Father."

"Why can't you just take a rifle? He wouldn't miss it at night."

"That would be like stealing."

"All right, I'll tell Captain Feher," Peter said. "We meet at ten sharp, beyond the village, by the stone cross. Get yourself some dark clothes." He climbed the fence and began to run. I went back down to the house, to my room to ransack my wardrobe. In the end I decided the dark brown Red Indian suit and moccasins Mother brought me from Paris would do. I spent the afternoon cutting off the red felt fringes.

I got out of bed, already dressed, at a quarter to ten, pulled on my moccasins, and left the house over the bridge. I didn't need to be especially quiet, for the grownups were singing. I recognized Mother and her friend Anna, the opera singer, yoo-hooing at each other in a duet. I climbed the fence by the second terrace. From somewhere Solomon came to see me off.

In ten minutes I had reached the main street of the village. It rose slightly here as the road curved over a stream. I crossed the bridge. Below me tiny silver crosses vibrated on a motionless black ribbon. Most of the houses were dark. Somewhere a drunk began to sing.

27

As he passed the houses, the village dogs, one by one, started to bark, until a woman's shrill voice cut the singing short. The invisible drunk cursed; then a door banged shut. The frogs took over again.

Even before I could see the stone cross I knew that they were already there. I felt it somehow, and I could smell them. The very poor, who lived in caves at the far end of the village, always smelled sour. I took two more steps and stopped. A torch thrust a white beam into my face; then I heard Mr. Feher.

"Boys, our gentleman guide has arrived." There were sniggers. The white beam dropped away from my face to the ground, making a narrow line leading to the cross.

"Come here!"

I went, wishing that Father was here with me. Nobody ever sniggered around Father.

"Good evening," I said. Again, sniggers were coming from the dark.

"I don't expect you to salute me properly like a soldier," Mr. Feher said, "but I warn you, we are not playing games. Now, tell me; is it true that you have been over?"

"Yes, it is true."

"Don't lie to me." He put the light on my face.

"I give you my word of honor." As I said this somebody laughed aloud. Mr. Feher turned.

"Shut up," he said. "Do you want to come with me, Laszlo?"

"Yes, sir."

"Good." He put his torch down on the base of the cross beside some flowers. They were soft and bent, dying. "I want you to write on this paper, Laszlo, that you come of your own free will. . . . Good. Another question. Have you anything in your pockets that would identify you?"

"No, sir."

"Good. From now on you'll be called Number Twenty-five. And you call me Captain Feher."

"Yes, sir."

"All right. Give him a rifle. The rifles are not loaded. I'll give the order to load."

It was Peter who handed me the rifle, an ammunition belt, and a bayonet. The rifle was an old .256 Mannlicher. We had two of them at home. I pulled the bolt back.

"What are you doing, Twenty-five?"

"I am checking my rifle."

"I told you it wasn't loaded."

"Yes, Captain Feher. My father told me I should trust only my own eyes and fingers with any weapon in my hands."

"Fall in!" he barked. "Extinguish your cigarettes. If I catch any of you smoking I'll smash his toes with his own rifle."

We started on the four kilometre hike in single file.

We rested awhile on the shore behind a large weeping willow. Two boats were hidden under the tree. Peter lay on his back beside me pretending that I wasn't there. I had fixed my sights with a white thread and reached for his rifle to fix his sights too, when Mr. Feher asked me what I was doing. I told him that Father had taught me this and that we always did it when shooting in the dark. Mr. Feher took my spool of white thread and threw it away, calling me a seamstress. I wondered if the others would talk to me now that I was called Twenty-five. They whispered among themselves.

A black cloud covered the stars.

"All right," Mr. Feher said.

We loaded our rifles and the boats were pushed out onto the river. Two men rowed in each boat. The oars dipped silently and we seemed to be floating above the water. In the dark I could smell everything separately: the trees on the shore behind us, the river, the men in the boat, our rifles, and the boudoir smell from the collar of my Indian blouse where my sister had once poured some of Mother's perfume.

"Are you scared?" Peter whispered into my ear. I shook my head. I was afraid of many things: our Latin teacher at school, the mad woman of the village with her large goiter and strange running walk, the whirlpool close to the dock where the head gardener's son had died; but there was nothing frightening in tonight. I was happy. Darkness was safe, Father had told me. One just had to lie down and keep still. I was safe here. And if I got shot, that would just make me more like Father. He had two wounds from the War.

"Watch your oars," Mr. Feher whispered in the

other boat. The denser blackness of the shoreline rushed out at us; then the first boat crunched on it. We came in much more quietly.

"Twenty-five," Mr. Feher whispered.

"Sir?"

"Who do you want to go with you?"

"I ask for a volunteer," I said. Father had silenced the Russian observation post with volunteers.

"Keep your voice down. Who wants to go with Twenty-five?"

Peter volunteered. I knew he would.

"All right. You go to the pillboxes, close enough to find out how they are manned, then come back and report to me. Understand?"

"Yes, sir."

"Leave your rifles here."

We moved slowly in the dark, like a war party of Indians. I could just feel the branches touching my face. Indians always knew where they were going, and they were patient. I knew where the pillboxes were and I was patient. I halted for a moment to listen. Peter bumped into me.

"What is it?" he whispered.

"Nothing. I was just listening."

"Go on, Twenty-five," he said. We went on. Soon I found a path. It was a shy, unobtrusive path, winding between trees and bushes. It felt safe walking on it. I began to jog, holding down the bayonet with my hand.

The trees suddenly fell away. The stars were out

again and the pillboxes were there, just across the field. I was looking at them, feeling exactly as Father must have felt when he crawled out from the trench knowing that the whole regiment watched him. The pillboxes were real, and I was real.

"You've seen them, Laszlo," Peter whispered. "Let's go back."

"What would Captain Feher do to you if we don't find out how they are manned?" I crawled out onto the field. I was completely soaked by the heavy dew. Peter followed me.

It was a long crawl. The muscles in my neck began to ache. I told myself I shouldn't mind because this was a part of soldiering. Then we reached the first pillbox and it was all right again. In the silence I heard the river. They were close to the shore, camouflaged by green grass to hide them from us on the other side.

The first pillbox was empty. Even the squat steel door stood open. There was no machine gun inside. We checked them all. They were all empty. I felt like a little boy playing at soldiering. I turned angrily and started back across the field. Peter pulled me down. Then I saw it too: a white house, further back inland on a mound partly hidden by trees. We took cover and waited.

"I hope they have no dog," Peter whispered.

"We can find out. You bark, Peter. You bark better than anyone I know."

"I can't. Not now."

We fell silent. A soldier appeared. I could see him

against the house. Then another. The smaller one lit a cigarette. They were talking.

"It's real. After all, it's real."

"Shut up," Peter whispered. "Shut up!"

The guards went on talking. I knew what to do. When Father saw the Russian observation post, he took one of his men with him and silenced the guards; then they surrounded it. The Russians came out with their hands held high and the Russian officer handed Father his revolver. Father offered him a cigarette. They shook hands.

The smaller guard pitched his cigarette away and disappeared behind the house. The big one lit up now, and shielding the cigarette in his hand, turned to go to the other side.

"We're going up there."

"What for?"

"To silence the guards."

"No," Peter said.

"We can't go back otherwise." The night had faded. The exposed side of the house had lost its clean contour and washed into the background.

"What'll we do?" Peter asked, eyes on the house.

"We'll go up there and silence the guards. I told you."

"Kill them?"

"We don't kill. I'll bang them over the head with the bayonet. Then you go back and get Captain Feher to surround the house and we take the Czechs prisoners." I started off walking, bent over. I was in a hurry, afraid that Mr. Feher might move up and spoil everything. He wouldn't know what to do in a situation like this. He hadn't been in the Great War. Peter followed me. At the foot of the mound we got down on our stomachs and crawled up to a position behind a tree. We waited.

The big guard walked by. He smelled of tobacco and soldier smell, but he didn't move smartly like a soldier. He went up to the front of the house and called out to the other guard in a loud whisper. An answer came back but not the little guard. He must have sat down behind the house. I was thrilled to hear them speak in a language I couldn't understand. This was real. Father had taught me to say 'hands up' in Russian, but I wasn't sure if the Czechs would understand Russian, and besides, I couldn't frighten them without a rifle.

The big guard turned and walked back. He came close by the tree, stopped and yawned, then went on. I stood up. Now he wasn't so much bigger than I. His back was very wide. I lifted the sheathed bayonet. He stopped again and leaned forward a little. It felt like bringing down an ax the wrong way. It jarred my arm. His cloth army cap fell backward, then he pitched on his head with a thud. His falling rifle made another noise. Peter came and dragged him down behind our tree.

"What'll we do now?" Peter sounded strange.

"Unsheathe your bayonet," I whispered. "Put its point against his heart. If he wakes up, he'll feel it and won't dare move. Do you know where his heart is?"

"Yes." He had the bayonet in his hand.

I crept around the house. The smaller guard was sitting on the ground, propped against a tree trunk. He looked little and tired, but he was armed with a rifle. I banged him over the head. He moaned. I lifted him under his armpits and dragged him around the house to our tree.

"Peter!"

He didn't answer.

"Peter!"

I let the little guard down. Peter was sitting beside the big guard with his head bowed, rubbing his hands on the grass. He was crying.

"Peter!"

"I didn't mean to do it. He moved."

"Peter, there are more of them in the house —"

"I didn't mean to do it."

"You must go back to Captain Feher and bring him here. Tell them to come quietly. There are more in the house."

"I can't go without my bayonet."

I pulled it out and gave it to him. He got up and left. I moved the little guard behind another tree and sat down beside him. I looked at his alien uniform. He was a Czech soldier. And so was the other. Enemies. Both of them. Czechs with sneering voices. It began to go round and round. I couldn't get off. I felt sick.

The little guard was sitting up looking at the naked bayonet in my hand. I didn't remember unsheathing it.

35

"Lie down," I said in Hungarian.

He lay down.

"You speak Hungarian!"

"My people were Hungarian," the man said, "but when I grew up this was already Czechoslovakia. . . . What happened to Ladislau?"

"He is dead."

The little man covered his face with his hands.

"He didn't mean to kill him. You must understand."

"We're not at war."

"He didn't mean to kill him."

The little guard didn't say anything.

"How many are there in the house?"

"Fourteen. What'll happen to them?"

"We'll keep them prisoner till we go home," I told him. "I am sorry that I can't offer you a cigarette."

"Aren't you too young to smoke?"

"Get up. I'll walk you past the house."

"I'd rather you kill me while I'm lying down," he said. "It would be worse walking away waiting for it."

"I'll turn you loose, but you must go away from here and not talk to anyone. There are more of us coming up soon and they might want to lock you in too. You must go far from here."

"I will."

"Give me your word of honor."

"All right."

He gave me his hand. It was calloused and limp and he was sweating. I don't know why but it made me remember the flowers on the base of the stone cross.

By the time I got back Mr. Feher was coming up the mound with his men. One of them gave me my rifle. The white thread was ripped away from the sights. They surrounded the house. Mr. Feher beckoned to me.

"You did a good job, Laszlo. Did your father teach you how to do it?"

"Yes, sir."

"You and I go in now." He took the gun from its holster. "You can learn a few things from me yet."

I clicked off the safety and followed him. He opened the door and stepped back. Nothing happened. We went in. Mr. Feher turned on his torch. There were men sleeping on cots ranged along one side of the room. On the opposite wall hung rifles. Mr. Feher grabbed the nearest sleeper and shook him. The man sat up and said something in Czech.

"Speak Hungarian," Mr. Feher shouted. The man just shook his head.

"Anybody speak Hungarian?"

I was covering them with my rifle. They didn't seem to want to get out of their cots.

"I speak Hungarian," a blond fellow said.

"Tell them that the house is surrounded. They are to get up and line up by their beds." The man translated. "Tell them to keep their mouths shut. . . . Why is there nobody at the pillboxes?"

"We are not at war with anybody yet," the interpreter answered. "We have no machine guns for them."

The fourteen men lined up by their cots. In their

37

underclothes they did not look like Czech soldiers. They looked like people.

"I want more light," Mr. Feher said. The interpreter lit a gasoline lamp and pumped it up. They were looking at us. Nobody said a word. The lamp hissed like an angry gander.

Mr. Feher called in six of his men.

"Two of you take the rifles and ammunition outside. The rest watch the prisoners. You come with me, Laszlo."

I followed him outside. He had not offered any cigarettes and he had not shaken hands. It was no honor serving under him. I wanted to go home.

"Laszlo, we have to plan the next step together. You'll understand what I am getting at. You are not a stinking peasant like my men." He laughed. I didn't say anything. Father would never call a peasant stinking.

"Are you listening to me?" Mr. Feher growled.

"Yes, sir."

"You knew how to silence the guards. You understand the necessity —"

"We didn't mean to hurt him."

"I expected a different answer from you. Do you understand that we can't take prisoners?"

"No, sir."

"What would you do with them?"

"I would keep them in the house with two guards. We can lock them in when we leave. . . . And I would free the man who speaks Hungarian."

"Why?"

"Because he is our brother. We don't want him to hate us."

Mr. Feher leaned against a tree and laughed. "D'you think it matters how he feels about us? The only thing that matters is who is stronger. That man is in Czech uniform. This isn't your father's kind of war. The Gentlemen's War lost us a big part of our country. Think about it."

He walked past me and called the men outside to gather around him. Morning breeze came from the woods. The trees sighed. I was sure he wouldn't do it in daylight.

"As I told you," Mr. Feher said, standing in the center of the half circle, "the Free Corps doesn't take prisoners. Our safety demands this. We don't ask for mercy and we don't give mercy. If one of these bastards escapes from the house we can expect the whole Czech Army at our back. We'd be lined up and shot." Mr. Feher waited. Peter glanced behind him. All the others looked behind them. It was morning now.

Mr. Feher went on. "I don't want to attract the enemy with rifle shots. It has to be a quiet job with the bayonet. One by one, like pig killing. Any volunteers?"

Nobody moved.

"I offer five pengoes, extra, from my own pocket."

"Number Nine humbly reports."

"All right," Mr. Feher said. "Number Nine, take up position by the door. The rest, line up facing the door. I'll make men out of you yet."

Mr. Feher went inside the house. We lined up in double order and waited. When he came out he stood in front of us, a bit to the side, and called us to attention.

"Let's begin," he commanded.

The interpreter came outside and the door shut behind him. His uniform was unbuttoned, his hair uncombed. He had forgotten to put on his cap. Seeing us, he stiffened.

"Did you tell them to come out one by one to be searched?" Mr. Feher asked.

"Yes, sir," the interpreter said.

"All right. Go ahead and search him."

The man lifted his hands high and waited. Number Nine stepped behind him. The bayonet sliding in between his ribs went so fast that he died before registering pain. Number Nine dragged the dead man's body to the side of the house. He cleaned off his bayonet on the dead man's jacket and went back to stand by the closed door.

"Next one," Mr. Feher called.

The door opened and a man stepped out. He lifted his arms high and waited. A question appeared on his face as if he were listening to a faraway sound. Then his knees buckled. Number Nine pulled him over beside the first one and cleaned off his bayonet.

"Next one," Mr. Feher called.

The door opened. A man stepped out and lifted his arms high. The door closed. He stood still, then his knees buckled. Number Nine worked with the not-too-slow, not-too-fast rhythm of a woodcutter.

First there had been a man's face and his disheveled hair. Then came the man whose face asked a question. The next one was not a man; he was an automaton, an automaton whose hair color and whose face I could not remember. Was he tall or short? The door opened and shut. It was a soft sound and the automatons kept coming, looking alike. There must be more to it because this couldn't be all; but they kept coming out looking alike. They all held up their hands before their knees buckled. I looked at the others. They stood at attention in their green Free Corps coveralls, chest out, hands flat at their sides, like soldiers. I too stood at attention, thinking of Father, the way he stood when the band played the national anthem but I couldn't do it right. The Indian suit was brown but it wasn't real because real Indians dressed in leather.

The sound was not angry, not like the time I slammed the door on my sister. My legs felt boneless and I looked down and noticed that I had left on two red felt fringes. I ripped them off. Nobody noticed and it made my knees feel better and it stopped me from hearing the soft sound. I counted up to twenty before it came again. The next time I counted very slowly up to thirty. It wasn't fair to count too fast. I looked at one of them because there must be more to it than this. I wanted to remember a face but all I could see was fear. I closed my eyes. I counted to sixty, then stopped because I had to take a breath.

"Next one."

The door did not open.

"Next one," Mr. Feher shouted hoarsely. "Next one."

The door opened and one of the guards came out. "There are no more in here, Captain Feher," he said.

"At ease!" Mr. Feher commanded.

We hid the boats under the weeping willow. All the time, rowing back, we had tried not to look at each other. Mr. Feher said that we were dismissed. He told us to disperse at ten-minute intervals. I pulled back the bolt on the rifle and took out the clip; then took off the belt with the bayonet and handed them back to Mr. Feher. He wouldn't take them. I laid them at his feet. He didn't say anything, just looked at me. I turned around and walked away.

On the highway there were always people coming and going and saying: 'God give you a good day,' so I kept to the shore. Soon I was out of sight of Mr. Feher and began to run. The grass felt good to my feet, and the sandy patches, and even the willows whipping my face now and then felt good. When I was a little boy my Indian name had been Swift Feet. Sometimes, to myself, I was still Swift Feet. I had been here only last week, jogging along at the wolf trot, feeling the same grass under my feet. I stopped running. I looked for signs as I walked by the Big Chief trees I knew, but they were the same as usual, tall and stately, the greatest among their people.

The side-wheeler Tahi was coming upriver. She

always came between ten-fifteen and ten-thirty. I couldn't tell time by the sun like Peter. He had learned it when he was young and took care of goats.

I passed the abandoned brick kiln and reached the backs of the village houses. I tried to think of breakfast; I tried to think of Trianon, of Injustice, of Our Brothers in Subjugation, of Honor. I tried to think of what Father had said about his return from the War, but I remembered only the tall chimney of the kiln, as it had come down two summers ago. One minute it stood above almost everything; then the supporting trestles at one side of the undermined base burned through and the chimney fell. First slowly, unbelieving that its time had come, still higher than the church steeple, then faster and faster, rushing down. When the dust settled, there were only broken pieces of brick scattered on the ground. I wanted to think like a soldier, but kept on thinking like me.

I took the short cut through the woods, running all the way to our high stone wall with its wrought iron gate. I was breathing so hard that it sounded as if I were crying. For the first time in my life I didn't know what I wanted to be. I could always pretend to be anybody I liked, but now I couldn't even pretend to be my yesterday me.

Solomon scented me and started a racket behind the gate. I went inside. He jumped on me and licked my neck, then went down to sniff around my moccasins. He was finding out where I had been. I took the left-hand stairs and walked along the first terrace. Everything was quiet. Mother must have taken the guests for a walk. I came level with the terrace and saw Father sitting alone in a deck chair under an umbrella, reading.

"Good morning, Father," I said, and walked past him.

"You must have been up early, Laszlo . . . Laszlo!"

"Yes, Father?"

He looked at me, then swung a leg over the deck chair and stood up.

"Anything the matter?"

"No."

"Let's go up to your room," Father said, leading the way into the house and up the stairs. He stopped in front of my door. I opened it.

"Come in, Father."

He came in. "You haven't slept in your bed," he said.

"No, I haven't."

"You can always tell me if you want to go out at night. We always trusted each other."

"Yes."

"When did you go out?"

"Last night."

We stood in the middle of my room. The polka-dot curtains on the window were fluttering like ducks just out of a pond.

"Where did you go?"

"I'd rather not tell you."

"I am asking you."

"I went over the river with Mr. Feher and his Free Corps."

He took a step toward me. "Is that man mad? Once a thing like that starts, God only knows where it will end. And you, going with them!" His eyes were hard but he kept his voice down. "What is the purpose of a Free Corps? To kill unsuspecting people, then run back home feeling like heroes? Tell me."

"To kill Czechs." When I said this, Father pressed his hand to his head as if he were slicking down his hair.

"Because Czechs are not people with four limbs as we are? Because they have no mothers and fathers and children as we have?"

I couldn't answer. I saw them again, standing in their underclothes beside their cots, looking like people.

"Have you . . . have any of the Czechs been killed?"

The plum tree outside the window was humming with bees. Cook was singing in the kitchen.

"Yes."

"What made you go with them?" His question was a great shout that filled the room, hardly leaving me any space to breathe.

"I wanted to be like you, Father."

He knocked me down. I waited on the floor, hoping that he'd bring his riding crop and beat me so hard that I could be forgiven tomorrow. But he didn't beat me. He picked me up from the floor and held me against his chest. I heard him murmur: 'Lord, what have I done?'

45

"You didn't hit me hard, Father. I don't feel it at all."

He didn't listen to me. He said it again, out loud now, and I felt his chest vibrate with each word.

2

The Binge

He watched his sister's tight grip on the receiver. It gave her hand the color of the winter apples they bombarded each other with as children. The sun coming through the curtains made her hair light up. The window panes were taped with large X-es. She put the receiver down.

"Bad?"

"He is dying," she said.

"I have to see him."

"You can't. The railway lines are bombed, and it would take days to get there." She was her practical big sister self. "You can't leave now. You have your orders."

"What can I do?"

"She asks you to pray for Father."

"Me?"

"She knows how I —"

"Yes," he interrupted, not wanting to hear his sister say it out loud, defining her disbelief, and so build a huge, empty edifice of hopelessness. They were both saved from saying anything more. Planes were coming toward Budapest and the air raid sirens began to moan.

When it was over, he went out to the street directly from the shelter. Halted yellow streetcars were dotting the main artery like prehistoric creatures mired in quicksand, already dead. He walked fast, conscious of his black riding boots, one of his father's special presents. Everything he had ever given him was special: the cigarbox truck his father made for him on his sister's birthday when he had felt left out; that 'If God is for us, who is against us?'; that Hungary was the most beautiful country in the world, yet it was conceivable that a French woman like their mother would think otherwise; the first rifle; they were all special presents because they came from him.

Somewhere, across the Danube on the Pest side, fire trucks and ambulances were screaming. With an almost automatic stocktaking, he once more compiled the list of friends living over there.

The church, antithesis of anything that might suggest Rome, stood close to a park of well-trimmed grass and tamed, captive chestnut trees in solitary confinement. Each had an iron fence around its base that reached up a few feet, making the trees look like giraffes in a zoo. Walking up the steps, it occurred to him that he had never really prayed for his father before. He was always included, but more out of politeness than a feeling that he needed to be prayed for. He simply and always WAS.

The church door was made of varnished oak. He put his hand on the wrought iron doorknob and turned it. The door was locked. He shivered with fright, his body seeming already to know what his mind would not accept, not yet anyway, casting about desperately like a starving fisherman only to come up with a wriggling poison fish. He turned and ran down the stairs, his boots noisily clomping, then dampened by the thick, orderly, Calvinist grass he passed the imprisoned trees, grinding now the gravel on the walk where trusting little boys, coming up out of their air raid shelters, played ball not knowing anything about the black cloud of predestination that had already marked them. He crossed the street, slowing down to a walk because people were looking at him, a lieutenant in the tank corps. He was twenty-one. He went on searching for an open door. A place for a rehearing, anywhere now.

A huge cross faced him, almost as if to bar his way. With abhorrence he saw the bleeding, twisted body of Jesus hanging from it, looking like the dead who were dug up after the raids. The dead Kristus as if resurrection had never been. Kneeling down — he who had never knelt in his life and who looked down on the papist, idol-worshipping, incense-burning majority of his countrymen and his own French mother with the amused tolerance of a Westerner meeting a prayer-wheel-spinning lama — he was not certain if he had not by this one act compounded all his sins into a super wrong.

"Our Father," he said; then he stopped. He wanted his own father. There was nobody who could take his place. "Don't take away our father, oh Lord God," he prayed.

Somebody came into the church. He got up and went outside, halted by the strong sunshine. He noticed the women in their summer dresses floating by him, their buttocks and breasts moving with tiny motions that took his breath away and caused his chest to ache with longing for all of them. Four more days, he thought, and I'll be sent to the Front. The perfect thing to say to a woman to be loved quickly. And it was the truth.

Away from the church a question mark grew into a snake that curled around his father's chest to strangle the beating heart. There was no more sun in the sky, no streets, houses, roofless walls with staring, empty eyes, no women, no desire, merely the endless grey ribbon of the sidewalk cut by chasms into which he stepped, deaf to the blaring of cars and the clanking of streetcar bells. *When people died under them they were covered with sheets of brown paper*. But he came up again and again onto the grey ribbon.

The incense smell didn't bother him anymore. It was cool inside and as soon as he knelt down, peaceful. Too cool and too peaceful for the questionmark snake to enter. He knelt silently. There was no need to say out loud: "Don't take away our father, oh Lord God."

He was resting safely on his knees. When he got up he was a happy man just recovered from a grave illness.

It did not last long. Like a drunk in search of the next bar, he stumbled from church to church, till, remembering the morning's raid, he crossed over the Danube to Pest. The morning's raid made the black smoke rise up straight, then rejected, bent under the clouds, grey now, then nothing. Air. Golden-blue summer air that had been a house with people in it.

They used to row a long way up the Danube. The green river was hemmed in on both sides by wheat fields. Golden-yellow. When a breeze was blowing they could smell the ripeness of the kernels and there was always a sound like a contented sigh.

The air raid sirens began to howl. The shelter he took was in an ornate 19th century apartment house. The helmeted air raid warden standing outside saluted him.

"This is a lucky shelter, Lieutenant. Glad to have you, sir."

"Thank you." Lazily he touched his cap, playing his role of a 'line officer home for a brief spell' for the warden. To keep it up, he one-two-three-foured the length of the stone floor, then down the grimy stairs to a narrow corridor formed by the dividing iron fence. The door hung open waiting for him. He stepped inside and stopped, forgetting his self-appointed role. There was an electric bulb hanging from the vaulted ceiling like a single fruit of a dried out, dead vine. It gave out shadows that turned people's faces into a set of bones. They sat on backless benches, each with a suitcase or a box as if waiting for a train.

"Sit down, Lieutenant," somebody said. He sat down among them and touched his face, feeling the bones. I must be like them, he thought. He watched an old woman lying on a cot with her arms folded over her chest. She looked at him and shivered. Without a bag, a box, or a suitcase he alone was naked. Nobody spoke.

Then the sound came. First like the susurration of tiny, feathered wings, then whistling with increasing frenzy till the bang of explosion shook the building. The light swung side to side like a railwayman's lamp. Another one. It walked on iron shod feet, shaking the earth, coming closer. In the dark a child whimpered.

Not much longer now, he thought, wondering how that other pain would feel.

The light came back on. A woman with her head on the bench was kneeling as if at a confessional, her bent back asking for mercy. The earth stopped shaking.

The All-Clear sounded. He rushed up the stairs, across the hall, past the warden standing at the door with his steel helmet hanging from his arm like a shopping basket, down the street, running by a caved-in house where people were digging with ineffectual frenzy. He stepped over a body that the explosion had smashed against a wall, the brain, flesh, blood and bones mixed in a pulp with bits of clothing. He went around a mountain of brick where a leg stuck out, bent at the shin. There was no street to go on. Turning back he walked slowly, for the first time noticing the thick white dust on his black boots. Uncle Joseph was bigger than his father but he fitted in an urn the size of a pound tobacco can. Ashes to ashes. There was nothing now. He walked on. As in a delirious dream he stepped on a street sign, halted, bent down, read it twice, went on, came back to read it again. It was the street where the woman in the wine-colored dressing gown lived, had lived two weeks ago, the two of them together. An urgent, hungry cannibalism on his part and a betrayal on hers that chance had arranged and that allowed him to shake himself dry like a dog coming in out of the rain, but now it was the only thought that did not hurt. He was running again, running toward an untouched house, through the hall, surrounded by echoes of his own footsteps. He stopped to push the dead bell, never for a moment doubting that she was there behind the door. He banged on it till the door opened and he rushed in not hearing her say: "What is it? What is it?" to hold her close, to feel her body against his.

"Let me close the door," she said, leaving him. "I thought I'd never see you again." She watched his face, his eyes, then she asked it again: "What is it?"

In four more days, he wanted to say, I'll be at the Front, but instead heard himself blurt out: "My father is dying."

"And you came here?"

"I saw the smoke in the morning." They were still standing in the narrow entrance like polite strangers, apart but attentive.

"You want me?"

He didn't answer. Just looked at her.

"You need me." It was a statement.

This time he saw her with eyes that wanted to memorize, photograph her ivory skin, her long limbs, her heavy breasts pulling away from each other, her face, one cheek buried in the pillow, showing her profile cameolike. Gently he turned her head, looking down at her closed eyes, her trembling mouth.

"I would like to stay with you always," he said. He noticed then that she was crying.

After he left her house, he stopped to phone home. His sister answered. Hearing her voice, he knew. He stepped out of the phone booth to look up at the sky and shout: take me, take. me, but his open mouth was mute as if his vocal cords had been ripped out. He knew that if God is for us who is against us, but if God was against you. . . . The soundless words asked for American planes and bombs and death. Nothing came. The sky was overcast that night.

3

Curfew

The windows of Comedy Theatre looked down on the street below. There was no traffic on the street. There was no glass in the windows.

A man hobbled by on mismatched canes. One was an Alpine walking stick, the other a ferrule-tipped ebony cane. He was dressed in black military boots and khaki britches, a pinstriped, double-breasted jacket whose collar was fastened around his neck with a piece of string and, as if to symbolize his peaceful intent, a black homburg. He turned right, into a narrow street where the houses leaned inward protectively. His walking stick sounded louder here, like a blind man's progress through a permanent darkness. Suddenly he stopped. Somebody had stepped out of the shadows.

"It's five to nine," the woman said.

They will kill me now, he thought.

"I said it's five to nine."

"Thank you very much," he said with a polite little bow in his voice.

"I am not the worst looking girl in the world, I can tell you that." She was offended. "And you have to think about the curfew too. They'll shoot you on the street after nine."

"I know," he said.

"Come up. It won't cost you much." She stepped closer to him. "You are crying."

"No," he said, "I am not." But he was crying.

"You just came back?"

"Yes."

"You are a soldier, aren't you?"

"Not anymore."

"Try and tell that to Them," she said and began to walk away. "We can't stay down forever."

He followed her.

The house had a big door. A man with a sad mustache opened it. He held out his hand, palm upward.

"He is my —," she was at a loss for the right word. "He is not a guest." She went up the dark stairs, looking back nervously at the soldier. It wasn't right what she was doing and she did not want the old man to think that she had gone soft in the head.

The second flight had wooden stairs. The soldier liked that better. They felt alive. The woman waited for him and he touched her hand. Hers felt warm and he wanted to put his whole body in it.

A small door led into the room.

"No electricity, of course." She lighted a candle. He completely forgot to miss electricity.

"You are younger than I thought," she said. This made him self-conscious. He was nineteen.

"It's a nice room," he said.

"You don't have to be polite, it's not mine. Take your clothes off. You are dirty."

He sat down on the bed and pulled off his left boot, then he tried the right one. He couldn't move it.

"I can sleep on the floor." He sounded so defenseless that it made her angry.

"You are dirty and I don't want any lice in here."

The soldier tried again, but it was too painful.

"I can't do it."

"I'll help you with it."

"It's ugly to look at," he said.

"You lie on your back and shut up. Ready?" She turned her back to him, his right boot between her thighs. He watched her and forgot to be ready for the pain. The barbed wire around his brain tightened.

When she saw the blood coming, she cursed and eased a pail under his leg then pulled off her dress and placed it neatly on the chair.

Under the pinstriped jacket she found his gun. She looked at it, thinking, then with two fingers lifted the gun and with the distaste of a little girl carrying a dead snake put it behind an empty flower pot. She piled his clothes into the bucket, poured water over them and placed it on the stove.

He was half asleep, listening for sounds beyond the door and to her moving about. He held his breath to hear better but it only made his heart drum inside his head. He wanted to open his eyes to see the candle light but sank down into deep darkness.

He came to on the bed, under a blanket, feeling strangely clean. The candle was extinguished but the room was not black and suffocating. The blanket pressed on his bad leg. He moved slowly, trying to see with his hand. He felt her body and it took his breath away.

"Are you sleeping?" he whispered.

"No," she said.

His hand moved slowly as if it wanted to memorize or remember something. She touched him with her thigh.

"Are you a virgin?"

"No." His hand fell on her breast. "Do you like this?"

"Sometimes." She thought for a moment. "Would you like to do it?"

"Yes." He forgot the outside world, even forgot her. "Yes." He felt with his hands, arms, whole body. There was no pain left in him, no fear, no tiredness. He moved unknowing, he moaned unhearing and then, he lay still. The blackness that covered him now was warm and safe.

"Let me get up," she said.

"Come back, please." He was lying on his back. She washed and came back. The bed creaked.

"I didn't think you'd want to do anything." She lay close to him. "Your leg is bad."

"I thought They would shoot me on the street to-night. But I am alive." He chuckled like a little boy.

"And you have a gun," she said.

He froze and she moved away from him.

"Have you ever killed?"

The soldier sat up and moaned. He had hurt his leg.

"Lie down," she said. "You should be proud of it." She lit a cigarette in the dark. He could see her hair for a moment. Dark blond. Soft.

"How did it feel?"

He got angry. "Stick a knife in a block of butter."

"Would you kill somebody for me?" She exhaled the smoke and put out the cigarette in a saucer.

"That was a stupid joke."

"A stupid joke because you are a little boy?"

"I was a soldier."

"Then kiss me."

He kissed her and touched her breast. "It feels good."

"Would you kill one of Them for me?"

"The fighting is over."

"Do you know what They did to women?"

"I know."

"Your nice girls sent them over here. Go to the whores, they said. They won't mind. Do you think a whore can't be raped? Do you think I can't be raped?"

"Don't talk, please."

"He is in the house, drunk as a pig. Some kind of an officer. They will never look for him here. We are

59

off limits. Put a blanket over his head and shoot him."

"What did he do to you?"

"He is one of Them."

The soldier sat up, his bare feet touching the floor. "I don't want any more killing."

"You are a coward. You cried," she said. He hit her face and got out of bed.

"Where are my clothes?"

"You can't have them. I boiled them because of the lice."

He hit her again. She cried now, aloud. Then they heard somebody running on the empty street. The steps came toward the house. She stopped crying. More running feet. The soldier stood naked by the window, watching.

The street was well lit by the moon. A man in a ragged, torn uniform was running on the sidewalk. From beyond the corner the sound of pounding feet came closer. The running man bumped against house doors, trying to get in, hitting them as an insect, attracted by light, hits the windowpanes. He crossed the street and headed straight for the door that shielded the naked soldier standing by the window. He stopped an instant and jerked the door frantically. The door remained closed and he ran again across the street. There was a house with only one wing of the door standing. He lunged toward it running even faster. The patrol, covering both sidewalk and the middle of the street, turned the corner. The running man looked back and jumped toward the house. A tommy gun burst, splattering the wall. The man fell, hitting the sidewalk with his head, then slid on his stomach toward the open doorway.

The echo of the tommy gun burst died down. Nothing moved in the silence. The man moaned and the patrol stepped out of the shadows and walked with efficient strides toward him. They stood around talking while one of them pried up the man's shoulder with his boot. The man's head turned, showing the other side of his face.

A single shot and the fallen man kicked out with both legs. The patrol moved on.

Some windows were carefully closed, then the street was silent again. The soldier standing naked by the window looked down at the motionless body spread out on the sidewalk.

"Come to bed. You'll catch cold," the woman said.

He came back. The bed creaked. He took her head in his hands and kissed her.

"Tell me your name," he said.

4

Brandenburg Concerto

He sat on a boxcar's floor with his legs outstretched, leaning against the wall wrapped in one of the Brandenburg concertos, feeling content. The music was alive and intimate and nothing else existed beyond it. It had been very difficult for him to start it playing in his head but once he could remember the sound of the Ruggieri violin, piccolo tuned, the rest came easily. By the time the concerto reached the first Menuet he swayed with the music, the back of his head rolling from left to right, right to left on the side of the boxcar. Even the crack around the sliding door turned white as if the music had become visible, bringing in light.

"Lieutenant," the girl, an ancient twenty-three-year-old bone collection with short, comical, dead hair, called to him, "How far are we from Budapest?"

"I don't know," he said, angry at her for shutting off the music. Now he had to limp with the rhythm of the boxcar and remember that just an hour ago, when the train had stopped, this same skin-and-bone creature had been raped by three Russian soldiers. They had pushed the sliding door back and climbed in flashing around with a battery light. One of them kicked him aside and then raped the girl. It would have been very simple had they not kept the light on the girl's face. Her eyes had been like glass eyes. Not frightened or accusing or anything. Just dead. "I don't know," he said again, feeling guilty for his anger. "I really don't know."

"I believe you, lieutenant," she said.

"Call me Peter."

"Thank you."

"What is your name?"

"Sarah. I am back from Auschwitz."

Auschwitz didn't mean anything to him. A town in Germany or Austria.

"Do you like Bach?" There was no answer, so he repeated the question. "Do you like Bach?"

"Yes," she said in a small voice.

"Are you crying?"

"No," she said. He reached out for her hand. A little, rough, narrow hand.

"You are crying now," he said, moving closer to her.

"I am lousy."

"Who isn't?" He put his arm around her bony shoulders and eased her head onto his chest. She didn't weigh more than a rabbit. "My mother used to enjoy just reading the score."

"I like Bach," she said, wonder in her voice. The snoring of the sergeant at the other end of the boxcar stopped with a moan. Peter could hear the music again. The limping rhythm changed to a pleasant swaying.

"Can you hear it too?" he asked. Then his heart jumped, but it was all right. She wasn't dead. She was just sleeping. Peter kept on swaying; then he too dropped off.

The noise of the sliding door being pushed back woke him. The sergeant was looking at him apologetically.

"I'm thinking of getting off, sir. It's not healthy for us around stations."

"I am in no shape to do any jumping, sergeant, but you go ahead."

"Sir!"

"Yes?"

"Just wanted to say, sir, that I am pleased to have served under you." He delivered his speech standing at attention. Peter squirmed a little. The girl was pressing on his leg.

"You were like an uncle to me, sergeant," he said, hoping he gave something too.

"Do you have your crutch handy, sir?"

"Yes. Don't worry about me, sergeant. They won't take a man who can't even walk properly."

"You'll be all right, sir, after a while, but I don't like to leave you."

"All right, sergeant, jump."

"God be with you, sir."

"God be with you."

Peter saw him drop from the open door. The limping rhythm was the same again, then changed to the minute thunder of a bowling alley as the train crossed another track, then again the limping. The variety of sounds made the train seem to go faster.

The girl woke up.

"We are almost at home," Peter said. "I recognized the rubbish dumps. They are still here . . ."

"What will happen to you when we arrive?" the girl asked, her eyes on Peter's right leg.

"I don't know."

"What's the matter with your leg?"

"It's my thigh. The fragment or whatever it is, is pressing on the bone. It doesn't hurt if I don't step on it."

"You'll have to go to a hospital. . . . I was a medical student before They took us away."

"Then you must be older than I am."

The girl ignored this. "Didn't you have doctors in the Army?"

"The doctors had no time to really fix it," Peter said. "We were pressed very hard. I was left behind to take care of myself." He looked toward the open door and added: "The sergeant decided to stay with me."

"He must have loved you."

"Who?"

"Your sergeant."

"He had enough of war."

"Maybe if you stay with me," the girl said. "I am Jewish and the Russians fought the Nazis."

"Stay with you?"

"You'll be safe."

"Safe?"

"Yes." But she began to cry. "I am a little bit crazy."

"Everything will be all right when the war ends," Peter said. "Where are your mother and father?"

"They are dead. Have you got anybody?"

"My mother and my sister, I think. We live on the Buda side. You can stay with us."

"Me?"

"Yes. You like Bach." They both laughed.

"You are good," the girl said. "I never thought. . . ."

"Thought what?"

"I never thought that I'd ever want to speak to you."

"Speak to me?"

"If you had been herded like . . . like. . . ."

"I was at the Front. I wasn't doing it. My family didn't approve. . . ."

"But you knew at least some of it. And you were not one of us when. . . ."

"That's true."

"I like you, anyway."

"You are a good Christian."

"I am not even a good Jew," the girl said. "I don't believe in a God who can let things like this happen. Can you?"

With loud clanking the cars bounced against each other like billiard balls; then, after a final convulsion the train stopped. The girl was at the door looking out, then the next minute the air was rent by the firing of automatic weapons. Peter, lying on his side, heard the girl shout: "What is it?" then voices answering back. Now there was firing all around them. The girl was kneeling beside him trying to get him up, but he wouldn't move, not as long as he heard the tommy guns' rattling.

"The end of the war," the girl shouted. He stood up leaning on his crutch, the sound of killing miraculously transformed in his ears into the happy sound of a Saint Stephen's Day fireworks. He hobbled to the door to shout with the others milling around the bent tracks, burned-out railway cars, and the patched-up skeleton of the station. People on their way home: Polish and Ukrainian girls who had grown into womanhood in labor camps; Jews, the skin-and-bone remnants of Auschwitz and Belsen; Hungarian men and women dislodged by war; and soldiers. Victors and vanquished, they all shouted and cried and kissed each other. Peter, standing in the doorway of the boxcar looking at them, felt love rising in him for all the people, his brothers and sisters, spared by the mercy of God so that they all could live in peace. The mementoes of the war were still there, but he had already stepped over the threshold where war, hate, and fear were left behind like bad dreams in the morning.

"I am hungry," Sarah said. The firing of tommy guns tapered off.

"So am I," Peter said. "Let's go home."

She helped him down and they joined the throng of people scurrying about like rats or sitting on their bundles, with infinite patience waiting for a train or the news of one that would take them home. A woman stepped in front of Peter, carrying a small photograph like a sick bird in the palm of her left hand.

"Have you seen him? He is my son."

"No, but don't worry, the war is over now."

The woman left without a word, her eyes already scanning the crowd for returned soldiers.

"Can you walk on?" Sarah asked. Peter was watching the woman stop another soldier. The soldier shook his head.

"Of course I can," Peter said. They walked across what had been the platform.

"I feel dizzy," the girl said, walking slowly beside him.

"We'll eat soon. It's the sun on an empty stomach."

"Water would help. You know when one drinks very slowly, pretending. . . ."

"Yes," Peter said, seeing for the first time the armed Russian soldiers around the station. They were not waiting for a train to take them home. "The war is over," he murmured.

"What?"

"The war is over," he said, noticing the blue visor caps of the NKVD and the torn uniforms of the Hungarian soldiers herded in one corner of the station.

"Peter," the girl said. "Peter."

"I see Them," he said.

"Stoy!" the command came. "Halt."

"We are almost home," Peter said, going on; then he stopped. He heard the click of a rifle bolt. Two Russian soldiers in clean, neat uniforms, holding their rifles under their arms like hunters, converged on them. The smaller one grabbed Sarah by her arm and pointing with his head outside the station said: "Davay, davay." The girl just stood there looking up at Peter.

"Davay! Davay!"

"He wants you to go home," Peter said.

"I have no place to go," she said; then, when the other soldier stamped the ground with his feet, she began to run. She ran like a stray dog, with her head turned back every third or fourth step to look at Peter. Once she stopped altogether but the soldier again stamped the ground and she went on running, her ankles buckling under her as she stepped on pieces of brick and cement. Finally she was out of sight, lost among the rubble. The soldiers laughed and good-naturedly nudged Peter to join the prisoners in one corner of the railway station. There were twenty-five of them from all branches of the Hungarian Army, a dirty, dejected lot, some of them without shoes, sitting or standing in little groups. As Peter hobbled closer to them a horse-faced artilleryman jumped up from the ground where he was sitting and rushed at him.

"This is an officer," he screamed. "Take him. I am a

proletarian. I want to go home." He spat at Peter. "See him standing here high and mighty? I am a proletarian I tell you."

Two men pulled him away and sat him down on the ground again. An NKVD officer walked up to Peter now.

"Do you speak German?" he asked, addressing him in German.

"Yes, I do."

"Where did you learn to speak German?"

"As a child I had a German nanny." The NKVD officer was now standing almost nose to nose with Peter. "You are lying."

"I am not lying."

"So you are not lying. It was the German nanny who told you to pretend that you are wounded?"

Peter didn't answer.

"Drop your crutch!"

The crutch fell with a clutter on the pockmarked asphalt platform.

"Walk!"

"I can't walk."

"Where are you wounded?"

"Here." Peter pointed at his right thigh where his riding breeches were slit to allow for the thick, dirty bandages.

"We'll see," the NKVD officer said and gave an order in Russian. Two of his soldiers came to stand on each side of Peter. "Walk!"

"I can't without the crutch."

"No?" He shouted something in Russian.

Peter heard a horrible, animal-like sound; then his head hit the platform. He didn't feel pain. He knew only that some warm liquid was slowly coursing down into his boot and remembered his father telling him that a gentleman always tries to avoid creating a scene and opened his eyes. It was blood. He felt a sense of relief; then his thigh started to throb with agonizing, tearing pain. Somebody gently kicked his good leg. A Russian soldier was bending over him.

"Davay," he said. Peter was pulled up and the crutch thrust into his right armpit. Standing once more he saw the NKVD officer unconcernedly smoking a cigarette and the prisoners huddled together like cattle in the wind. He wondered if he should not walk up to the NKVD officer and do something that would build up the men's morale, but a new dizziness made him forget the men and his duty. All he knew was that the crazy angle of the sky was threatening him somehow and that pain which had been contained in the sector of his right thigh burst through and took over the whole of his body.

"Davay," the Russian soldier said kindly, his outstretched arm pointing the direction. Peter went slowly, trying to keep the sky, now blindingly white and dotted with sharp, black dots, from turning over and pushing him down into the blackness of the ground. Concentrating hard, he hobbled on; one, two, one, two, his left boot kicking away broken bits of brick, one, two, his crutch writing a monotonous Morse code: one, two. He passed the line of armed Russian soldiers ringing the railway station and was among mountains of brick, splintered wood, and chunks of mortar. Crushed houses which had become hills with ridges and valleys and slopes, houses turned into burial vaults smelling of the sweet smell of death. The footpath opened into a street where houses stood, some listing, some shored up but standing. He hobbled on a sidewalk, noticing empty, glassless shopwindows where women and a few old men sat, two or three to a shopwindow, selling their wares. They looked at him with frightened eyes, in silence. One, two, one, two. There were other pedestrians on the sidewalk. Not running or crouching in doorways but walking. He had come home. One, two. . . .

"Good, fresh hard rolls," somebody called out. Peter stopped, dragging his crutch upright. The woman was sitting in the shopwindow, next to a laundry basket full of hard rolls. Hard rolls used to be served for breakfast on white plates, sliced in two, ready for butter and jam.

"I didn't mean to," he croaked.

"It's all right," the woman said. Peter jammed the hard roll into his mouth and went on. One, two, one, two. The shopwindows and the people in them were weaving from side to side. Tick, tock, tick, tock. There was a grandfather clock in the dining room. The pendulum swung between ivory columns. One, two, tick, tock. He felt the dizziness coming again. Where was he? Where was home in this disfigured, bashed-in, strange city? It used to be a long way from the railway station, suitcases cramping his legs as the cab drove past three bridges, then turned left by the monastery with its many sweet bells, and crept up a steep hill to a quiet, tree-lined street. There were no taxicabs, not even street cars. One, two, one, two. A building was missing here, then shopwindows again and people in them. Tick, tock, tick, tock. An old man wanted to give him a cigarette, but Peter couldn't stop now. The house was far away and the sun got brighter and brighter. The black dots were coming back, making his heart race madly. One, two, one, two.

He was standing in front of a shopwindow seeing the glinting, jagged edge of glass in the black-burned frame. The dusty wooden floor was partly covered with a sheet of brown paper. A woman was sitting on it with a basket on her lap. There were cornmeal cookies in her basket. Bright yellow, he could see that clearly. The woman was wearing a calico dirndl as if dressed for a costume ball. There was something wrong with her. They were looking at each other. Her eyes were brown and shaped like his own and she was crying, sitting there with the basket on her lap. Then she lifted her arms.

"I won't be able to get up, Mother," Peter said, sitting on the brown paper beside her, not hearing her say: "My son," and explaining that she had been waiting here every day for the past three months, knowing that he must come this way because she had prayed. He couldn't hear anything. His ears were filled with the noise of eating the bright yellow cookies.

74

5

Brindley

The milk cow bellowed. She must have gone to the barn, to her stall. It was Sunday. I didn't want to get up just yet. A half hour more wouldn't hurt her bag.

"Time to get up?" Meg stirred beside me.

"She can wait a little longer today." I don't think Meg heard me. She often asks questions or talks politely in her sleep. Like the time when the horses pawed on our front steps. That was six months ago when we first came and before I'd put up the barbed wire fence around the house. The horses — three of them — came one night, banging on our steps with their hooves. Meg, still asleep, called out, "Come in."

That was a long time ago, an unbelievably long time ago. Then our home was only a shell of a house, with no water or bathroom, and the tin roof curled up whenever the wind blew a little harder. Now we had, from the outside, a nice, clean, green-painted ranch-house with white window frames; and inside, a large one-room studio divided from the kerosene stove and refrigerator by a bar made of cypress. The walls were all sealed. We even had a bathroom, and running water which we couldn't drink. The water tower had no roof.

Lee slept on the porch, and played all day in the pine woods surrounding our house. She was safe there with her cats and sometimes, when they were not busy, with my two cow-dogs.

Life on the ranch was hard work, especially the first few months when, after working twelve or fourteen hours outside, I went on building, with Meg's help, the inside of our house. But it was worth it. I felt healthy, capable, powerful. The feeling of power came from the two hundred and fifty head of stock, and from the fact that the boss only came once in two weeks, staying a day. Only just lately he had talked about an arrangement making me into something of a junior partner. I could hardly remember a time in my life when I felt so secure and could think without fear of tomorrow. There had been a time. It took place in another world and now had the quality of a fairy-tale.

Suddenly the milk cow bellowed, close to the house. She had come up to make sure I could hear her. Lee who slept on the porch woke up and, standing on her bed, talked through the screen to the cow. Meg woke up too.

"I'll have to bring Lee in," she said. "It's too cold

on the porch if she isn't covered up."

I got up, washed my hands in the ice cold water, washed out the milking bucket; counted out the drops of disinfectant into the bucket and poured some water in. Meg brought Lee in, put her in our bed, and started dressing. I picked up the bucket from the sink and went to the door.

"I'll be back."

"I am glad you reassure me." We said this every morning and it always sounded funny. The nearest neighbors were five miles away.

Once outside I stooped under our rope gate and walked on the narrow path through the pine trees to the barn. The milk cow, whom we called Rishka, cantered behind me, making happy noises in her deep voice. She was the only one on the ranch who was fed the special dairy feed, and she was well aware of this. At the barn I opened her stall, put down the milking bucket and went to the feed room. I measured out her portion into a bucket and closed the door.

Rishka was waiting for me in her stall in front of her box. I poured the feed in. She pushed me away.

"Do you want me to kick you?" She was not interested and went on without a pause with her feeding. I reached for the milk bucket and the one-legged stool.

Sitting beside her I washed her bag with the mixture of disinfectant and horrible cold water, then dumped out the rest of the mixture from the bucket and started milking. Rishka felt warm. The noise of the two thin streams of milk hitting the bottom of the bucket sounded with the sure rhythm of a slow-moving steam engine.

I liked milking. This was the time when I could dream or write poetry. I never put those poems down on paper. They were beautiful in my head, and escaped the scrutiny of words committed to paper.

The first few weeks milking had been no joy, especially in the evenings. My hands got painful cramps. Then I dreamed of milking contests in which I always won. My method was unbeatable. I needed only to hold the cow's tit and the milk flowed out just as water flows out of a turned-on spigot. After a time the cramps left my hands and I never again won milking contests.

Rishka finished eating and turned back her head, looking at me.

"I'll just strip you dry. You won't have to wait much longer. Don't look at me."

Rishka sank her head in the feed box and with her tongue sandpapered it. I stripped her dry, picked up the bucket, and kicked the stool into the corner. Whistling, the Seaboard Line train passed by the far corner of the ranch. It was seven o'clock. Late for milking, but it was Sunday.

Rishka, moving slowly, headed for the Pensacola-Bahia pasture. I walked back toward the house. From among the trees out stepped Mr. Grey and settled himself silently but squarely in my path.

"What the hell do you want? I have milk in the bucket. You know that. You feel like being a calf again? I tell you it's milk in the bucket. Let me by. Listen, Mr. Grey, if you don't move in a second, I'll kick your nose."

Mr. Grey did not move an inch and I did not kick his nose. It would have been ridiculous to try to show him who's boss. Mr. Grey was a huge, humped animal, by nature and profession a Brahma bull. He was gentle, but persistent. Once he pushed the feed room door, and me behind it, inside. I could only scare him on horseback.

I walked up close to him.

"I'll let you sniff the bucket just for once. You can see for yourself it's milk." He let me by.

Time after time Mr. Grey or Brindley tried to intercept me after the morning or evening milking, expecting feed in the bucket. Brindley, though almost as big as Mr. Grey, was never a real problem. He had no guts. He was a steer. There was something curiously sad about Brindley. He made me feel uncomfortable whenever he focussed his red-rimmed, hesitant eyes on me. Brindley looked like a lush out of money, asking for just one more drink.

I bowed my head under the rope gate. I didn't need to open and close it all the time, and it kept the cattle and horses out just as well as a real gate would have done. The cats mobbed me, and the dogs started to howl in their enclosure. I went inside the house.

Fire was burning in the little trash-burner. Meg stood by the kerosene cook stove fixing breakfast. The smell of kerosene was strong, but it didn't disturb us anymore. It was as much a part of our lives as the sand around us.

"We need some more wood for the burner," Meg said.

"Shall I go now?"

"No. Your breakfast is ready."

I sat down by the bar. Lee, holding on to the wall, circled around the room till she reached the end of the bar, then holding on to it, came to me. She put her head on my leg, not unlike one of her cats.

"When you go out for the wood you can take Lee with you. I need peace to clear up the house." Meg handed me a plate full of pancakes.

"Have you eaten?"

"No, but you just go ahead. I don't want you to faint."

The dogs outside in their pens were barking in a frenzy.

"I'd better take their food out. I don't want them to faint either."

"Finish yours first . . ."

The dogs kept howling. I poured honey, cut up with my fork, and swallowed. We ate well on the ranch, and the memory of my bean diet seemed, from the distance of a full stomach, quite humorous.

I finished and took out the dogs' plates. The cats mobbed me and the dogs were jumping high inside their pen. I kept them there part of the time so they wouldn't run down all their weight. As I stepped inside the dog pen, Shan the collie sat down in his corner as I had taught them, but Fritz the German shepherd charged at the plates.

"Fritz, you idiot, sit down." Fritz sat down, shaking. He was the younger of the two and needed more talking to. I gave Shan his plate, then Fritz got his. He ate with terrific speed, all the while watching Shan and growling. Fritz had had a bad home. He'd starved most of his puppy life.

I went back to the house for the cats' milk. They took care of the rest of their menu. Meg helped me carry the plates outside. We set one plate farther aside, then I went back for Lee and put her beside the plate to guard it from the other cats. The plate belonged to Toby — a shy creature who only trusted Lee. His mother, we found out, had been shot in front of him.

Toby came crouching low over the ground, his bushy tail straight out behind him. He stopped and froze a few feet from his plate. Meg and I went inside and watched Toby from the porch.

Toby still stood frozen a few feet from his plate. The other cats, almost finished with their milk, eyed the one full plate.

"Toby," Lee called, stretching her little hands toward the cat. "Toby." Toby moved closer, his tail still straight out behind him. "Toby," Lee called again, and Toby dipped his nose in the plate.

The other cats left their empty plates and formed a semi-circle around Lee and Toby. When Toby finished his milk he walked straight into Lee's arms, gently miau-ing.

"Keeleecat," Lee said, pressing Toby to her chest.

"Lee has appreciative friends," Meg said. "But I do wish she had some children near."

"She sees Julie almost every Sunday."

"Yes, but is that enough?"

I didn't know. We drove a hundred miles, round trip, most Sundays to see Lawrence, Nancy, and Julie. Julie was lonely for children too. At first, before we built our bathroom, the Sunday excursions supplied our weekly bath, as well as the only congenial company in I don't know how many hundred miles. We talked about everything under the sun with the pleasure of people understanding one another. The best, though, was Lawrence reading his book which he had finished, or — supposedly for the children — T. S. Eliot's poems about cats. His reading of "The Merchant of Venice" made me pity Shylock. I'd always hated him. The ranch was our life, but we thanked God for Lawrence and Nancy.

"Are we going this Sunday?" Meg asked.

"No. Not this Sunday."

"Anything special you have to do?"

"I thought when Lee has her nap, we could ride out. Sort of playing land owner and his lady. Stupid, isn't it? . . . To talk about the ranch. Something like reading a book together."

"You don't have to convince me so hard."

"You know, Meg, people who love each other should live the way we do. From the distance of the ranch,

82

people look much better. I couldn't have lived like this before I met you."

"I am happy anywhere with you," Meg said.

"You are the most beautiful, sweet, and interesting woman in this world."

"You are prejudiced and I am glad you are. I am also the most practical woman in the world; we need fire wood."

"Sorry. I forgot. We'll be back in an hour."

I found Lee outside the fence talking to some steers. When I picked her up, the steers moved away slowly, stopping and looking back every few steps.

"Pretty cow," Lee said.

"No. Steers. They used to be bulls." This sounded so funny to me that I laughed out loud. Lee found it amusing too and soon our sides were aching from laughing.

"We have lovely times together, don't we? Your father is a most witty guy, I must say."

"Daddy," Lee said.

"Can't you call me father? It sounds better."

"Daddy," Lee said.

"If you insist."

We walked to the dogs' pen and turned them loose. They both ran straight to the truck, competing for the first place, and jumped up at the same time. I opened the cab door and put Lee on the seat.

"We ride together in comfort. You can watch me drive."

"No." Lee said.

"What the hell do you want to do?"

"Go back."

"You have no right to ride in the back. You are not a dog or a feed sack. I'll let you go if you promise me to sit down. All right?"

"All right," Lee said.

I put her between Shan and Fritz and pushed the axe as far from her as I could. Getting in the cab, I set the mirror so that I could see her, and started. Fritz was affectionately licking her neck. We overtook the same curious steers.

"Pretty cow," Lee shouted. Shan growled.

"Shut up, Shan!"

Shan stopped growling, his tail beating on the cab. I reached back to pat his head. He licked my hand.

Close by, some cranes marched slowly on the St. Augustine pasture like orderly grey ghosts. Under a pine a cow lay tiredly. Her new calf stood on wobbly legs beside her.

My happiness was a physical thing. I felt it swelling in my chest, in my throat, in my lips which knew only one way to express themselves; to kiss this world of back-aches and post hole diggers, barbed wires and cut hands, new born calves and circling buzzards.

Monday, here, was not grudgingly different from Sunday. Monday did not mean a last-minute hated scramble in congested traffic. Just as five o'clock did not mean the end of working or responsibility. One clocked in coming to the ranch, and the clock kept on ticking. If it stopped, it stopped for good. The days were the same whatever their name might be.

By the time the train went by the ranch, I'd hauled all the needed fertilizer to the clover pasture and filled up the "Eezeeflow" for the first run. I pulled it with the jeep, fairly fast, which almost shook the hell out of me. Some cows with calves came from a farther pasture to watch, perhaps hoping that I'd leave the gate open to the clover field. There was no starvation on the ranch, with the supplementary feed, but the cattle were not overfed by any means.

Up and down the clover pasture the jeep was bouncing, rubbing my back on the back rest. If I slowed down, the skin on my back burned as if after a severe sunburn. This was not as bad, though, as the sudden jolts, jarring my insides. I couldn't slow down for long. I had no time. After I finished with the fertilizing, I planned to dig for water. The barn needed whitewashing, fences needed repairing; more land to be cleared and put into grass. I speeded up.

Two more turns and the "Eezeeflow" had to be filled up. Then up and down again across the clover pasture the jeep bounced.

At mid-day I unhitched the jeep and drove back to the house for lunch. Meg was ready with the food, and Lee and I sat down by the bar.

"How is it?"

"Shaking me to pieces, but I'll be ready in a few hours."

"How long do you have to keep them out of the clover pasture?"

"A few weeks. The old man wants to get rid of the steers entirely and get some new stock. I think the clover is for them."

"I'd miss Brindley."

"Darling, we shouldn't think of them as individuals going to be killed. It won't do for a rancher and his wife."

"I know. But don't you feel bad about Brindley?"

"Brindley," Lee said. "Pretty cow."

"Yes, Meg. I even feel bad when he looks at me with his red-rimmed eyes. I can't change this. He is a steer and will be eaten."

"Sounds horrid," Meg said.

"Shut up, Meg. I want to eat in peace."

"I am sorry."

"I am sorry too. I am sore. The damned jeep rubbed me sore."

"Can't you slow down?"

"I have no time now. Don't worry. Later, when we build this up to be a big operation, we'll have help to do this kind of job."

"I'm happy as we are," Meg said.

"If we don't grow now, something is wrong with me."

We finished eating. Meg brought coffee.

"I'll go to town after lunch," Meg said. "We need supplies."

"Bring some sixpenny nails for the chute, please."

"All right." Meg was writing on a slip of paper.

"And the mail."

"The first thing I always collect."

"Well, take care of yourself. This is a very dangerous time in town."

"Don't worry about us."

"I can't help it. It's the tourist season."

"They aren't as bad as that," Meg said smiling.

"Meg."

"Yes."

"We ought to try to accept things as they are. Brindley is a steer."

Meg came over from behind the bar and kissed me.

At three o'clock I finished fertilizing and drove the jeep back to the barn. Seeing our car in front of the house, I walked over to get the nails.

"Any mail, Meg?"

She came outside.

"Lee is sleeping. Don't shout."

"I finished the clover pasture. Any mail?"

"No letters, but a cable from Hungary."

"It can't be anything special."

"No," Meg said. "It can't be anything special. Open it."

I opened it. It was written in Hungarian and at first it did not register on my brain. To my ears, unused to them now, the words sounded as though someone was hitting on a tin plate with a wooden hammer. I read it again. I did not translate it into English now and the words resounded inside my head. From my head they seeped down to my body, to my limbs, to my hands and feet. Words flip-flopped from the top of my skull down onto the brain, the uncovered nerves.

"What is it?" Meg asked.

As I told her, thick white clouds enveloped me, and my voice was too loud in the silence. The cloud stayed around my head, shutting out the sounds of the country.

"Can you hear anything?"

Meg didn't answer.

"I'll be back soon."

I was surprised that my hands could open the car door, and then could start the car and turn it round.

I left the ranch, but I didn't remember opening and closing gates. The highway was empty and straight, but I drove slowly. I didn't want to hit a bump in the road, knowing that this would jar the cold rock embedded in my chest. I sat straight, breathing carefully. The rock should not be moved.

The silence was remarkable. And my hands which drove so well through nameless towns. I wondered where we were going.

The car stopped at last on a red clay road. From the house Lawrence came out, walking toward the car.

"Andre! Are you all right?"

"Yes." I was all right. The cold rock was safely stuck in my chest.

"Anything happened to Meg and Lee?"

"No."

"Come in the house. I have some sherry."

"I can't come in."

"Why did you come then?"

The rock started sliding. It hurt terribly.

"Why did you come, Andre?"

"I didn't know I was coming here." The dislodged rock turned hot, burning my eyes. "My mother was killed."

A few days later the boss sent me a postcard telling me to round up the steers, put them in the enclosure close to the chute, and "finish them" up with special steer-fattening feed.

It was late afternoon when Meg gave me the card. I wanted to get it over with so I dropped my other plans for the day and went for the mare. I caught her with a bucket of feed.

I rode by the house. Meg came outside.

"Take the jeep and go up to the chute, Meg. Hide the jeep behind the chute and open the gate to the finishing pasture. When you see us coming, stand so that the steers will go in. O.K.?"

"Sure."

"Thank you. Don't be in a great rush. It will take some time before I get them up there."

I rode up on the mound not far from the house to look around. The mare hadn't resigned herself to work and was jumpy. From the mound I could see steers grazing in bunches. Further away, close to the woods, Mr. Grey, his cows, and calves were busy with the grass.

I lifted the reins. The mare started walking. I patted her neck. It was sweaty already.

We circled the steers slowly to get behind without jumping them. The bands edged closer to each other, moving forward toward the unseen chute.

I suddenly remembered that mother told me once that she wanted the "Love Death" from "Tristan and Isolde" to be played at her funeral. Or was it something else? I couldn't ask her any more. . . .

I started whistling the Pilgrims' Chorus behind the string of steers. They moved into a slow trot. I gave them the direction by moving the mare to their right or left flank.

We went through the sparse woods around our house smoothly, hardly ever slowing down. Meg had remembered to lock the dogs in. Then on to the dirt road between the fenced St. Augustine and Pensacola Bahia pastures.

Some stray steers joined the procession. I rode at the back, guiding them toward their death.

I wanted to think of Heaven — a place where mother and father are waiting for me; a place of reunion. I couldn't. Death had no meaning. The one thing I felt was its horrible claustrophobia.

I saw Meg in her red jeans behind the chute, holding Lee in her arms. The gate to the enclosure was open. The one steer inside must have walked in of its own accord. I recognized him. It was Brindley.

I drove back in the jeep with Meg and Lee after

turning the mare out.

"Brindley walked in just after I opened the gate," Meg said. "He was standing close by."

"They are all in. I never thought it would go this easy."

"You have a way —"

"Oh hell —"

At the house Meg made coffee and we sat down.

"Andre," Meg said. "Did you know that faith is not only for telling 'thou shalt not's,' but to give you comfort?"

"Meg —"

"I am not preaching. I don't even say it gives you strength. It gives you comfort. You need comfort."

"You are my comfort, Meg, as long as you are. This is life, Meg. I see it as clearly as I know that Brindley will be killed. We can't help this. Even if we could, we wouldn't do anything to stop it. He is a steer; he shall be eaten."

"I want to read to you from the Book of Job," Meg said. " 'There the prisoners rest together; they hear not the voice of the oppressor. The small and the great are there; and the servant is free from his master.' It's peace for her, Andre."

"There is something else to tell me, isn't there, Meg?"

"Yes. A letter from your sister. You know already about your mother. The details can wait. It can hurt you more."

It did. "You are the last one," my sister wrote. "You

must live to tell your children about us so that we may
live too. Istvan was taken last night. Remember our
talk, sitting on the black cherry tree? You were right.
It's not so nice to be grown up. God be with you, Old
Warrior, and wish me luck."

She didn't sign the letter.

A buyer came with the boss the sixth day after I got
the steers in the enclosure. The boss was in a festive
mood even though prices were nothing like last year's.

Taking the mare, we went to the enclosure where I
was told to cut out the steers they would point out to
me and drive them into the chute. First they wanted to
get out the "A-1 meat."

I got the mare inside the enclosure, closed the gate,
rode to the chute, and opened the gate connecting the
enclosure and the chute.

"The one with the red marking," the buyer pointed.
He looked like a comedian in his city clothes with
high-heeled fancy cowboy boots.

I cut out the one with the marking and ran him into
the chute. I remembered him. He used to fight the
others when I gave them feed. The next one was a
black, squat animal, close to the ground. Perfect. Once
he had cut his leg on the barbed wire. The cut festered
with screw worms. Meg helped me put the medicine
on.

One after the other I ran the buyer's "A-1 meat" into
the chute.

"How many you got in?" the buyer asked me.

"Thirty-nine head."

"Let's have one more. That one. The cracker with the red freckles." They both hooted with laughter. The cracker with the red freckles was Brindley.

"O.K." the boss said.

I closed the chute and got off the mare. The buyer's first truck arrived and backed to the ramp at the other end of the chute.

"Get in the chute and move them," the boss said.

"Young feller," the buyer said, "Try this one. It's one of them electric ones." He handed me a short rod, the size of a policeman's billy.

"I don't need anything. Thank you just the same." I went inside the chute.

The narrow end of the chute leading up to the ramp was closed. The lane was not more than four or five feet wide, the plank wall about six feet high. This gate at the end served to stop the cattle after a truck was filled up. I couldn't open it as someone had nailed it in. I turned around and walked back to get a hammer.

"I told you," the buyer shouted to the boss, "It works like greased lightening."

I heard the half-choked blaring of a frightened animal, then the pounding of feet, clashing horns, and bodies pushed against wood. In an instant the air was filled with sweetish dust. I saw Brindley pushed into the lane by the others. His head was turned sideways, but even so his horns caught on the planks. When Brindley saw me he threw his body backward, but nothing could stop the advancing fear. A man yelled.

Like a new tide the steers swept Brindley toward me. On me. I reached for the top plank. I was pulling my body up when Brindley's horn hooked my leg, dragging me down. Hands grabbed my wrists from the other side, holding me tight. My body was taut in the air. Then something snapped in my back and I didn't feel my legs anymore.

The driver of the truck and the boss pulled me over. I lay on the ground outside the chute.

"Can you get up, Andre?" the boss asked worriedly.

"Sure. I'm all right."

"Don't you want to rest awhile?"

"I'm O.K."

The sky was a blue dome completely covering the earth. There was no escape. I couldn't move.

In the shadow of the porch Meg packed the red wooden trunk. She finished, closed the top, and came over to me.

"It's all packed now. We can go any time you like."

"Where did you tell the boss to take our luggage?"

"To Lawrence's. There is room in their house."

"I wanted to go around the ranch for the last time."

"Why prolong it?"

"It is finished once more."

"This is no tragedy, Andre. You'll be all right in a few months. Till then you get paid forty dollars a week."

"And wear a corset all my life."

"It's only because the ligaments are not healed yet.

The disk and your hip are back in place but you have to be careful not to dislocate them."

"Help me up, Meg."

She pulled me up from the bed. I could walk now, but my torso felt top-heavy as if my lower spine were made of rubber.

"Where is Lee?"

"Outside, saying goodbye to the cats."

"What will happen to the dogs, Meg?"

"A man is coming over this afternoon to take them away until somebody takes over here in a few weeks."

"To live in our house."

"Didn't you enjoy fixing it? Even if we don't live in it?"

"I built it for ourselves. It was to be our home."

"The new people will enjoy it. At least they'll be saved from camping and overwork."

"Did you turn out Rishka's calf?"

"Yes. And I opened the gate to the clover pasture. The horses are in it."

"They will eat so much that nobody can catch them."

"The new people will manage somehow. Don't worry about the ranch anymore."

"Because I have enough of my own to worry about?"

"I didn't say that."

"I am scared, Meg. Before, I always thought nothing real bad could happen to us because I was strong and could get a job. Even digging ditches."

"Don't be scared. You have a few months to re-

95

cuperate, paid by the insurance. It will be all right."

"What will happen to the cats? They were Lee's friends."

"I don't know. Let's go, Andre. You shouldn't be up too long."

Meg helped me down the front steps. Five of them. We used to sit there watching our garden, or the cranes march by, or the antics of the sad little school-boy-looking Brahma calves. There was always something to see from the front steps.

Lee ran to me, embracing my legs. "Daddy," she said.

Lee had finally learned to walk. One day she just got up and walked.

Instinctively I bent down to get under the rope gate. The pain in my back was like fire.

"You shouldn't bend, Andre."

"Help me straighten out, Meg."

"Where is your brace?"

"I left it under the bed."

"You have to have it on when you walk. Just for a few months. You could dislocate everything. Just till the ligaments mend."

She went back for the brace. I opened my shirt and trousers. She put it on and laced me in.

I got in the back of the car. I was not allowed to drive. I couldn't push the pedals. Lee sat in front with Meg.

"It would be a joke if you stuck in the sand now."

"I won't," Meg said. "We are going."

Meg drove in low gear. I lay back on the seat and shut my eyes. I didn't want to see the ranch left behind gradually.

Over the drone of the car's engine I heard Lee's small voice shout happily: "Pretty cow, pretty cow."

6

Once You Were No People

The land rose only a few feet, but in Central Florida this was enough to turn the scrub palmettoes into the threatening crest of an ocean wave. The man leading the way carried his son's .22 presumably against snakes — it was closed season — though he knew that there was little chance of meeting anything. It was too hot even for snakes but he would have felt foolish tramping in the field without a firearm in his hands. This feeling, like the heirloom cufflinks packed in his immigrant's suitcase, had survived a four-thousand-mile journey. The man stopped to look around.

"Do you recognize the pines, John?"

"I think so, Daddy," the boy said. He was a stretched-out ten-year-old with hazel eyes, dressed in jeans, boots, and an old shirt. Like his father he wore his hair long but it was much lighter in color.

"Shall we rest?" the man asked.

"You really want to?"

"Yes," the man said. "Let's sit down over there."

Two scrub oaks stood close together. Their combined shadow lay on the sand with the casualness of a discarded, threadbare mantilla. It covered the boy but the man's legs were in the sun.

"I like the smell of guns," the boy said, touching the rifle.

"It's only a mixture of oil, metal, and wood," the man said quickly. He remembered some half-read chapters on the effect of early influence. "They stink."

"But you like this stink, Daddy."

"Yes," the man admitted. "And so did your grandfather. He showed me how to clean a gun properly."

"Like you showed me?"

"Yes, though your grandfather was much better at it."

The boy did not hear him. He was up and running somewhere. He came back with a flower in his hand.

"Sabatia," he shouted. "I never saw one before."

"How do you know that this is 'sabatia'?"

"Mummy and I looked it up in her flower book." The boy sat down again. "See the yellow eye?"

"Yes."

"And the short calyx?"

He didn't see it. "Yes."

"That makes it a sabatia. There are several kinds."

"Very good," he said, thinking that at the same age his own dream world was filled with heroes, wars, dead enemies, and his own dying. Life was a great heroic charge and a solemn military funeral. Everything else was only a preparation for it. The boy was safe, at least safe from himself, because he loved growing things. Covertly he looked at his son.

". . . Dr. Dickinson got his Ph.D. at Cornell," the boy was saying, "and that's why I should go there too, but I don't want to leave you. Cornell is too far from here. I'd rather not get a Ph.D."

"How old are you, John?" The man sounded patient and long-suffering.

"Ten. It was you who said time flies."

"Only the time that is already behind you," he said. "Not when you are waiting. Who is Dr. Dickinson?"

"You know him, Daddy. The old gentleman at church who sits in the third pew on the right-hand side. He is a botanist."

"Humm," the man said.

"You should talk to him, Daddy."

"I have."

"I mean really. You have a lot in common."

"We have?"

"Yes. The Communists kicked him out of China and he had a big medal from Chiang Kai-shek," the boy said, watching a woodpecker alight on the trunk of a scrub oak and lean back like a champion water skier.

"I have never been to China and the Generalissimo never gave *me* anything," the man said. The boy patted his arm reassuringly.

"You know what I mean, Daddy."

"Yes." The man pulled up a leg, opening a straight, dry riverbed in the grey sand. He lay there — a seventeen-year-old Free Corps man behind a machinegun — because his father died a hero's death at the beginning of the war. He lay there waiting for magic to happen. Somebody passed him the bottle again. He drank, corked the bottle and put it down next to him. He looked through the sights and saw one of Them coming, then another and another. He watched Them coming, ants growing bigger and bigger and felt the saliva dribble down his chin.

"Yes, I know," he said. "Did your Dr. Dickinson crouch behind a machinegun, drunk, not knowing what he was doing! Did he —"

"Daddy! He was a missionary in China."

"He was? . . . Then why did Chiang Kai-shek give him a medal?"

"Because of his bull," the boy stated matter-of-factly.

"His what?"

"Bull."

"A bull?"

"Yes," the boy said, explaining in gallons and pints how Dr. Dickinson's bull improved the Chinese cows.

"One bull?"

"Yes, Daddy."

"Must have been a fine one," the man said. He leaned down and kissed the top of the boy's head. "And he didn't even have a Ph.D. from Cornell." He was laughing and though the boy did not understand

102

the humor, he joined him and they waved from side to side as if suddenly they had turned into wind-blown sea-oats.

On the pale, hazy sky, black specks appeared and the boy stiffened. The man put his arms around him, knowing that he was back again in the fragment of a particular day; caught in it as if caught in a small trap that broke his leg yet allowed him to live. It had happened after three o'clock, after school. The boy was in a victorious mood, talking about the pass he had caught and run to a touchdown. They had been almost home, almost turned off the highway when they saw a circle of black specks that rose slowly like pieces of burned paper, that rose up and outward like some terrible cone imprisoning a motionless white shape on the ground. No, he thought, it's only a shirt, but they were there and he had to stop the car. He got out and touched Dapple's head and her beautiful, lithe pointer's body still stretched in a semblance of running, then lifted her in his arms. The boy, who had sat in the car bent forward, now raised his head and looked at him. He looked at him and began to cry.

"See that vine?" the man asked, standing up. His khaki trousers had turned dark-brown around his waist where he sweated.

"Yes, Daddy."

"With two shots it could be cut in half."

"I am not sure I can do it," the boy said, getting up. A sudden breeze made the palmettoes scrape each other. There was a click and the boy lifted the gun to his shoulder.

"A little bit to the left," the man said, slapping a mosquito. The boy fired again. "Now it's perfect."

"You shoot, Daddy," the boy said.

He lifted the rifle, embracing it for a moment. He had loved the P-38 Walther best, not just because of the way it felt to his hand or because it took the place of a protective, faithful dog who always followed him, but because there was nobody else to love. The heaven of his childhood was closed, his father was dead, his brother was dead, and he didn't know about his mother. The house had a direct hit and there was nobody to ask to find out if she was under the rubble or had got out in time. Perhaps she was out shopping for potatoes or was out for some reason he could not think of now because he was too tired and hungry.

I will shoot one for myself, he thought, standing behind an overgrown bush near what had been his home. Gun in his hand, he watched a well-dressed civilian approach in the greyness of early evening. A good suit could be traded for food, food that might last two weeks. Two weeks eating. Every day. And maybe getting drunk on a full stomach, which is so different from heaving and retching liquid and emptiness. The civilian walked slowly toward the overgrown bush. It was almost time for a Russian patrol. He heard steps coming from behind him, rapid female steps clicking on the walk, then muted where the asphalt had been blown away, then clicking again. He put the Walther away and turned around. The woman was walking with her head down. When she noticed him she shied like a skittish horse and stopped. He watched her looking at his dirty uniform.

"I have no lice," he said.

"You don't remember me, do you?" the woman asked. She was small, much like a porcelain figurine. "I used to see you on the bus before the war. Once, when you had your motorbike you offered me a ride but I wasn't dressed for it."

He bowed, feeling the Walther pressing against his stomach. "I saw our bathtub on the sidewalk," he said. "It wasn't hurt. It wasn't hurt at all."

She touched his arm. "Would you like to stay with me? You shouldn't be outside after dark."

He stumbled on the threshold, then the light went on, and the woman closed the door behind them. A piano was jutting out from the corner taking up most of the room. A table and a few chairs stood to one side.

"Sit down," she said. She placed her newspaper parcel on the table. "I play the piano for the Russians. They pay me in food."

He reached for the bread and bacon. The bacon was rancid but taste was not important. He had to fill the emptiness, to push it out from the inside before it would cave in. He began to gag but kept on eating, trying to fill the terrible black cavity inside him.

The sound came gradually and he felt it on his forehead like the beginning of rain, then he was drenched, immersed in it and he knew that it happened to him, that the deaf could hear again. The light went out.

"There is no electricity after ten," she said. "Coal shortage." She went on playing in the dark. He wanted to say something, he wanted to identify himself, he wanted to say: "Debussy," but instead he heard himself saying: "My God, my God."

The next day the Russians did not want music and the woman, whose name was Livia, stayed on the sofa because she was hungry. The day after that he went out in the early evening to conceal himself behind the overgrown bush. He stood there not blind or deaf anymore, knowing that starving to death was the better alternative, but it did not work. Then he tried to think of the dead man he had seen in a pasture because he was worse than all the others. He was worse because the grass was deep green and the cows stood peacefully grazing around him. There was a hole in his neck covered with flies. He tried to think of the long finger-nails and the yellowish hands lit up by a spring sun but all he really remembered was a grasshopper landing on the dead man's back. It sat there rubbing its legs together, then jumped away, high and far. He stood behind the overgrown bush with the lifted Walther in his hand, thinking of Livia who had given him all the food she had. He thought of Livia, who now lay unmoving on the sofa, and watched a well-dressed civilian walk toward him.

He fired and with a quick movement pumped the rifle and fired again. The vine parted.

"I'll never be able to do this, Daddy," the boy said.

"I am much bigger than you are. I don't have to fight the weight of the gun. . . . Let's go back to camp."

They started off toward the pines through bushes that tore at their clothes and poked them with sharp, boney fingers. The man looked back for a moment and saw that his son had a halo of gnats around his head.

"It's no use trying to shoo them off, John, but of course if killing a few makes you feel better, swat at them."

"I'm all right, Daddy."

They entered the pines. It was cool there and silent. Their boots slipped on the soft, rust-colored pine needles.

"Your grandfather used to tell me to take deep breaths in the pine woods because it was good for my lungs."

"Is it true?" the boy asked, taking a deep breath.

"I don't know, but it makes my lungs happy."

"Mine too," the boy said. "Daddy."

"Yes?" The man stopped.

"I would like to ask you a question."

"All right."

"Daddy, I was just thinking . . . Daddy, if you'd seen that it wasn't an accident, if you'd seen that Dapple was killed deliberately, would you shoot that man if you had a chance?"

"Yes," the man said full of anger.

"Shoot to kill?"

The man was listening for a sound, any sound but

nothing came. Then outside in the sun a grasshopper blasted off.

"Yes." He took a quick step toward the boy. "But you know that this isn't what He wants us to do."

"I know."

"Nobody taught you to hate. . . ."

"Some of the children in my class hate the President, and Mrs. Thompson said that. . . ."

"But the laws don't hate in America." He stopped. How could he explain to a ten-year-old the difference between hate as a human failure and hate sanctified by law? How could he explain his own belief and at the same time his terrible anger? "If I didn't think of the Lord," he said finally, "I would be even worse than I am. Can you understand this?"

"Yes," the boy said. "'I have not come to call the righteous, but sinners to repentance.'"

"Let's go on." He started off with long strides, carrying the gun under his arm.

"Daddy."

"What?" He turned his head like an impatient cart horse.

"Are Hungarians tall people?"

"No. I was extra tall for a Hungarian but I am just right as an American."

"Do you think I'll be as tall as you, Daddy?" The boy came around and stood in front of him.

"Height doesn't mean a thing. For some sports you have to be small, for others large. It isn't one's size that matters."

"What does matter?"

"We'll never get back to camp," the man said. He turned and walked away from the boy, thinking that what mattered was that you had the strength to be a gentleman, but this he could not tell him because something had gone wrong with the word or the concept of it, turning it into a silly whiskey advertisement. Then he remembered and stopped.

"Did I ever tell you about Mr. Jefferson?"

"Yes." The boy came to a halt beside him. "He kept his stables hidden under his house."

"There is much more to him." The man was irritated.

"I know," the boy said. "He built a copying machine, the University of Virginia with serpentine walls, and he gave his slaves rum because that was better for them; but he drank bourbon like you, Daddy."

"John!"

"Yes, Daddy?"

"You still didn't. . . ."

The boy interrupted.

"I know about the things Mr. Jefferson signed because they are our American heritage, but, Daddy, everybody knows that."

The man gave a wordless groan and walked on. Sometimes there was no use talking.

Soon they were out of the pine wood. The heat that merely shimmered now turned into an unbearable pulsation. It filled his ears with a drumbeat that got faster as he pushed his way through bushes and scrub palmettoes. He kicked into a cactus and the sharp pain steadied the drumbeat to a dull thumping. With the last few steps he came to the edge of the rise where the grey-white, brush-covered sand began to roll down toward an unused irrigation ditch and he saw a tree that lay in it, dead and rotting yet still reaching up, and beyond that, a wall of greys and greens and browns tangled into the solidity of a final curtain that had just come down.

"Daddy."

"Yes?"

"Is this the way back to camp?"

"Yes," the man lied. "This is the way back to camp." He began to march, unhurriedly yet with the precise, terrible forward movement of a military machine. He marched down toward the trench, then over the fallen tree which should have remained only a fallen tree. He entered the tangle and felt the briars cut across his cheek. His anger rose and blindly he began to fight vines and briars, dead branches and saplings which stood in close formation like a regiment on parade. Where was mercy? He watched his brother Arpad wave to him from the cockpit of a big transport plane loaded with paratroopers. The right engine fired up, then the left. Arpad waved again and the plane began to taxi slowly, then it turned into takeoff position. It started to roll faster and faster, its engines roaring. It lifted off the ground. He watched the plane climb, then for an instant stop in mid-air. Slowly the tail pointed down and it began to slip back. He heard people screaming in the plane and the engines' high, whining pitch. He was running toward it, his own voice superimposed on all the other sounds, calling on God. The explosion silenced everything. He was still running, feeling the heat of the orange flames, then he fell. Somebody was on top of him. He fought, hitting out blindly. He heard the ammunition of the plane go off in bursts and people above him saying, *you can't do anything,* over and over again. He was dragged away, then he was on his feet, stepping out with his automatic one, two, three, four, one, two, three, four, marching away from something blank and meaningless toward dots and shapes which turned into people. One of them gave him a ride into town, then he was walking again carrying his deaf and frozen body down a strange street, around cordoned off, charred houses, around a standing wall with a sink attached to it on the third floor level and underneath, where the second floor had been, a big seascape in a golden frame. Then he was climbing over a mountain of bricks and saw a half-buried cross and the fragments of a church steeple.

"Daddy!"

Where was mercy? He pushed and pulled but the trees did not give way, the vines constantly regrouped, and even the soggy soil conspired to hold him. He turned around. He was alone, lost, surrounded.

"Daddy. . . . Come this way, Daddy. I hear a car."

He could hear it too, changing down for the rise where the road bent, a mile before it came to the camp.

He followed the boy through an opening in the woods where he didn't have to tear down things in order to move.

"We were behind the road all this time," the man said, "walking around in a circle."

"We were lost, Daddy, weren't we?"

"Yes. Were you afraid?"

"No," the boy said. "I wasn't alone."

The thought came so suddenly that he had to stop. *Alone.* Standing there with the boy, he could see it now, clear and timeless. There was mercy. The Lord had come through Livia and the others, the people whose names and faces he couldn't even remember. He wanted to tell the boy, but there were no words because he realized the only common ground between him and his own son was a language about objects. Out of his limitation and his knowledge, he reached out.

"John."

"Yes, Daddy?"

"You know who wrote this: 'Once you were no people but now you are God's people; once you had not received mercy but now you have received mercy'?"

The boy glanced over his shoulder. "T. S. Eliot?"

"No, St. Peter."

"He was a nice old man."

"Yes, he was," the man said, thinking that Peter had more faith than most and was crucified upside down.

They strolled toward the camp on the short grass, smelling the freshly cut hay and the asphalt of the

112

highway. Directly overhead the sun was blindingly white. Grasshoppers took off like rockets, flew in an arc, landed, then took off again.

7

A Slow, Soft River

The girl was driving the car up the slope, bouncing over the ruts gouged out by the run-off; then stopping a second, she waved. The man and the boy didn't look up from loading supplies in an old wooden boat half floating on the Itchetucknee. The river was cold and clear and smelled of the fish that swam close to the bridge, their heads pointing upstream. They were silver or black, nothing in between, with tails going like slow metronomes.

The girl turned onto the highway. When the man heard the car crossing the highway bridge he lifted his hand and wiggled his fingers in farewell. The boy waded into the river. Hunching over the transom with the outboard, he looked like a stork fishing.

By next year, the man thought, he'll be taller than I am. The boy was sixteen and he forty-five.

"Daddy," the boy said, straightening up, "we are ready to leave now."

"Sam," the man called. "Sam."

From under the bridge a big, gaunt black and tan hound sauntered down to the boat. He had a false joint in his hip that made him drag his right hind leg. He came to the man and put his muzzle in his hand.

"Samuel," the man said. He felt love rising in him like a great shout that spread over the giant water oaks, the face of his daughter in the car framed by dark hair, her emerald eyes smiling goodbye, the wind on the pale green sea of the river with its island-pools of blue, his tall, strong son; and Sam. Sam who had been found two years ago in a Georgia swamp on the verge of death. He lifted his arms as if he wanted to breathe in the blueness of the sky.

"Praise the Lord," the boy said matter-of-factly. "Get in, Daddy."

"Do you feel it too?" The man was astonished as if the boy had suddenly spoken in Chinese.

"I don't know why I shouldn't. I'm normal."

They floated under the highway bridge, then shot through the culvert under the railroad tracks. There were some houses on the left bank, but nobody in them. The river turned and widened. A congregation of ducks bobbed on the ripples. They were white ducks with one blue-wing teal in the midst of them. Out of sight a heron sounded deep bass. The ducks tuned up. Then as if the conductor had come in, there was a

116

sudden silence. Sam stood up in the boat and, lifting his head, bayed.

"That was an otter," the boy said. Some turtles plopped into the water, one after the other. Sam lay down again.

"I feel the same as when I listen to Bach," the man said. "I am lifted up, I am soaring, and I am almost bursting with joy. . . . But it is all orderly."

"You can't orderly-burst-with-joy," the boy said.

"We better crank up." The man was looking ahead where the Itchetucknee ran into the Santa Fe. There was a large object caught in the turbulence, coming up and going under again like a drowning man.

The engine started with a shriek, then the boy slowed it down to a pleasant purr. They went around the obstacle. Close up it was only a tree trunk that turned with a nice even speed. A roller in a well-oiled machine.

The Santa Fe was wider and darker and so swollen that it hardly moved between the banks of moss-covered trees. The boy speeded up. Two long waves left behind by the boat rushed the banks like charging cavalry, then broke up into shiny fragments among the tree trunks. Dry land was nowhere in sight. The man turned his head to the other side. A new charge just broke among the trees, flashing here and there like pieces of broken mirror. Without warning he saw his friend Stefan on the hospital bed with his eyes half closed as he had been the last six weeks, breathing through a hole in his neck, his chest heaving. Then

117

the sun came out, illuminating the spaces among the trees. The green patent-leather leaves of a huge magnolia reflected the light upward.

A garment of praise for the spirit of heaviness, he thought.

The boat changed direction, then got back on course. The boy had just finished taking off his shirt.

"Aren't you cold?"

"I wouldn't have taken it off if I were," the boy said.

"Vanity," the man said. "You want to get tanned, somebody else wants to bleach out. It's all vanity."

"If we all have it, you must have it too, Daddy."

"I have it moderately. On some Sundays when it is cold enough to wear my suit which I got to go to England in, I think, aha, not bad at all, but your mother will say: 'It's all right if you don't put on any more weight.' And I quit saying 'aha' till next winter."

"I remember when you bought that suit. I was five years old."

"That can't be."

"It was when I was starting school in England."

"And I am still not famous," the man said, "but at least I can get into my old suit."

"You look great in it, Daddy."

The man accepted this with a slight bow. He remembered how he stood in the door of the intensive-care unit not knowing if he should go in, conscious of his good suit and the nurses who were looking at him. But it didn't last long, this male pride, because he saw

Stefan and understood that the rhythmic clicking he heard came from a green plastic pump attached to a hole in Stefan's neck. Stefan was pale, his unseeing eyes half open. For a crazy moment he had almost expected Stefan to ask him to have something to eat or to drink wine. He always did. But there was nothing other than the sudden awful silence of the pump. He was holding his own breath, wanting to share the pain; then the pump started and Stefan's chest expanded. The rhythm of the pump was back for a while, then it stopped again. He had reached out and laid his hands on Stefan's head.

"Do you want to fish?" the boy was shouting over the noise of the outboard. "Now that the sun is out I can see the fish." He cut back the engine.

"They prophesied rain," the man said, "but it doesn't look like it. . . . I'll just sit and watch you fish."

They anchored under a large oak. The boy cast; the bait falling like a meteor plopped into the river. Sam checked the sound. The boy reeled in and cast out again. Some ducks came in over the trees and settled on the Santa Fe.

"It's good to be away from the world," the man said.

"This is the world, Daddy." The boy reeled in again.

"I am glad that at least Sam can't talk back," the man said. "I am talking about this place where we can see and smell the sun."

"Yes," the boy said.

"I think it's all right for us to be here."

"Why wouldn't it be all right? We can't do anything for Stefan except pray."

"Even so, I saw Stefan at the nursing home and you didn't. There is no pump beside his bed now and that awful clicking is gone, but in a way it is worse. He struggles for each breath, and when I squeezed his hand there was nothing. In the hospital at least he squeezed back and I always thought of it as Stefan in a sunken submarine answering my knock, saying: 'I am here, I am here, I can hear you.'"

"I looked it up," the boy said, putting on his shirt. "The veins contract first to prevent too much bleeding, but if they don't relax after a certain time that part of the brain dies."

"Stefan was just lying there sweating," the man said, not smelling the sun, the river, and the fishes anymore, "and his pillow showed the damp outline of his head."

"I don't want to think of him that way," the boy said. "I always see him playing golf standing on that very green grass." He cast, the line flying out toward the other shore with a satisfying sound. The man saw Stefan, but he wasn't playing golf. He was sitting in his living room, in his dark green armchair next to a large candlestick with papers strewn around him on the carpet. Just two hours before the stroke.

"No bother at all," Stefan said. *"While I read it you eat something. And have some wine."*

"I have a nibble," the boy whispered. He leaned

120

forward tensely, watching his line. "It's a bite, real heavy."

Play it, the man wanted to say, but he didn't say anything. The boy was a fisherman; he wasn't. He remembered his own fishing in the Danube with a cane pole and the dozens of fingerlings he pulled out from its olive-colored water. He also remembered his father's smile that said: this is all right for a little boy but men, our kind of men, hunt.

"A fighter," the boy shouted, reeling in and letting out the line again. "A fighter." The fish leaped clear of the water then went down making the reel scream like an ambulance. "I am pulling him in now," the boy said. He turned the reel, his torso leaning forward in the attitude of a Protestant at prayer.

"I'll help you land it," the man said.

"I can manage, thank you." He stood up and lifted the fish into the boat. The fish, it was a bass, fell to the floorboard with a thud. The boy took out the hook. The bass kept on flapping on the board, then lay still. The man was watching its gills pumping in and out, in and out.

"Let's turn it loose," the man said.

"Why? It's a perfect eating size. It must be at least five pounds."

When the boy was younger, he cried easily. The look he gave now was a man's incredulous stare. I couldn't tell him, the man thought. Besides it would be all wrong. Pagan. An exchange with the god of the river.

The fish flopped once, then lay still. Suddenly it lit up as if a light had been turned on inside it.

"It's beautiful," the boy said. "It gave a good fight."

By carefully navigating among the cypress knees and tree trunks, they reached the shore under a bluff. In the silence of the switched-off outboard the tea-colored waves sounded like heavy breathing.

"I like to look down on the Suwannee," the man said. "This is how a flying heron sees it."

The boy laughed. "A two-hundred-pound heron. You would need a steel reinforced kingsize nest."

The bluff's floor was flat and covered with dry grass and the contorted trunks of live oaks. Sam checked out the place by circling around it. The man set up the tent. The boy chopped wood, built the fire, then neatly arranged his cooking tools on a stump.

"How do you feel about fish soup?" he asked.

"With plenty of paprika," the man said. He walked down to the edge of the bluff and looked down on the Suwannee. Its color alternated between royal blue and green with the edges saffron. There were no boats going in either direction. Some ducks dove, then bobbed back to the surface. Sam came to stand against the side of his knee.

"Sam thinks this is a good place," the man said. He saw Stefan's saffron colored shoes that he still wore even after shaving off his guardsman mustache and returning to his more conservative look. "I might get a crew cut," Stefan had said. "That would make me avant-garde now." But he didn't. His hair was damp and matted on the pillow. "A nice full head of hair," the nurse had said.

"Do you want to taste the soup, Daddy?"

It tasted perfect and he slurped another spoonful. "Who is to put a price on the joy of sitting here tasting your fish soup?"

"Some rivers had to be dammed up because people needed electricity. You can't damn progress, Daddy."

"I don't. I wouldn't be here without it. I was pretty badly shot up in the war. It isn't that at all."

"We can eat now," the boy said.

"Anything for Sam?"

The boy gave the dog a few uncooked hot dogs. The man watched the dog. When Sam ran he looked perfect. Only walking and sitting showed his crooked hip joint. We are both here, the man thought. It could have ended for Sam in that swamp in Georgia and for me at the border, under the barbed wire.

"Benedictus, benedicet."

"Deo gratias," the boy answered.

After washing up, the man climbed back up the bluff. He put the cooking utensils away and sat down on the blanket in front of the tent. For the last six years he and the boy had left on their annual boat trip on the Thursday before Easter. On Good Friday they would have a service of their own and be back at church on Easter Day. But this time it was different. He couldn't wait another day and he needed the strength of his son. The boy was whole while he was bruised and battered, only hoping to be made whole. The boy knew that with God everything was possible; he only hoped.

"John," the man said, "let's have our service today. It's because Stefan . . . we are out here and he —"

"I thought about it," the boy said. He stepped into the tent, got the prayer book, and sat down on the blanket.

"You read," the man said. "I left my reading glasses at home." He loved to hear the boy read, and besides, his own accent made him uncomfortable knowing that it would ruin something precious. The boy opened the prayer book.

"Now before the feast of the passover, when Jesus knew that his hour was come that he should depart out of this world unto the Father, having loved his own which were in the world, he loved them unto the end —"

The man listened, already thinking of tomorrow when He would be led to Pilate and shame and rejection and torment so that he, sitting here on a dog-smelly blanket, could be made clean and whole again.

"— For I have given you an example, that ye should do as I have done to you." The boy closed the prayer book. "Lord, we lift up our friend Stefan like those men who took the roof apart so that You could see their friend. You know what to do. We don't. Thank You."

"Amen," the man said, feeling peace carrying him

along like a slow, soft river. He knew that he didn't have to worry about Stefan anymore.

The boy put away the prayer book in the tent and came back with a cigar.

"I didn't know that you were smoking. That cigar's at least six months old."

"I don't," the boy said. "Stefan taught me to blow smoke rings. They would float beautifully out here."

This time the man didn't ask the boy if he felt it too. He looked at his watch. It was four-thirty.

Just before dusk, the boy, who was fishing sitting in the tied-out boat, called him. There was a snake swimming across the river from the other side.

The rain began at noon Friday, and it was still raining when they pulled out the boat at Fannin Springs. The wood around the boat ramp smelled like mushrooms. There were cars crossing the battleship grey bridge at long intervals, messengers from another civilization. In the pause the only sounds were the rain splashing on the Suwannee, the river itself, and Sam's running on the wet leaves.

The boy was stacking up the camping gear with an economy of movement. He had done this so many times that he could do it with his eyes closed. The man was standing facing the bridge, waiting. He was happy. The trip was accomplished, to be cherished and savored in detail and compared to other trips till next year when another would be added. He was waiting for his wife to come with the car and boat trailer, waiting with the same gratefulness to catch a glimpse of her face as he had waited long ago in an English church. There was peace in this waiting, a healing where nothing of the bigger world intruded so that when in time he would turn on the car radio he would not be crushed by the hate and despair.

"Here she is," he said. The car rumbled across the bridge, the empty trailer bouncing behind it. The trip was over. "John, go and back it down for her."

He watched them embrace; then the boy got in the car, turned it around, and backed it down. She was walking toward him with Sam, who had joined her. In his happiness he didn't notice the tightness of her face, only that she was glad to see him.

"You haven't changed," he said.

"Why would I change in two and a half days?" She put her arms around him. "You smell like a wet dog."

They loaded the boat and the gear and were off. It began to rain harder, coming down in grey sheets. The bridge rumbled under them, then they were on the highway. The boy was talking, telling about the trip from the beginning — the way they shot through the culvert under the railroad bridge and about the flock of ducks with one blue-wing teal in the midst of them. When he came to the fish he caught, the man remembered Stefan.

"How is Stefan?" he asked, interrupting the boy. He wasn't worried about him. He asked almost out of politeness. Even when she touched his arm he wasn't prepared for anything.

"He is dead," she said.

He heard the boy say "no" and his own fist crashed down on the steering wheel. The pain in his hand was the only feeling he had in the general numbness until he began to think and anger filled him against himself, against the river, against Thursday when at four-thirty he and the boy sat on a bluff hearing and feeling and trustingly celebrating like two madmen in the wine cellar of a bombed-out house. Then everything stopped. He drove on, peering through the windshield, noticing the curve in the road, an abandoned shack, a forlorn cow with her calf at her side. He marveled at himself that he could go on driving when life had lost all meaning because if Stefan was dead then God was dead also or He never had been in the first place and he had lived his own life for the past twelve years in a mental ward, hallucinating. There never had been a dialogue, a blessing and saving, a Body and Blood, and he was alone in an existential nightmare.

"There was no way I could contact you, and Jane wouldn't let me anyway," she said. "The women were in the room praying when suddenly Stefan sighed and relaxed. He was gone. He died on Thursday at about four-thirty."

Relief came with a rush and with it the accustomed and bearable seasons of joy and sadness all marching toward glory that was and is and ever shall be.

"Forgive me," he said. He began to cry.

G2